Issue Eleven
Summer 2016

YOUR IMPOSSIBLE VOICE

www.yourimpossiblevoice.com

Managing Editor: Keith J. Powell
Prose Editor: Stephen Beachy
Poetry Editor: Karen Biscopink
Feature Editor: Nicholas Alexander Hayes
Associate Prose Editor: Kate Folk
Associate Editor: Taylor Fredericks
Associate Editor: Alana King

Board of Directors:
Keith J. Powell
Stephen Beachy
Karen Biscopink

Contact:
email: editor@yourimpossiblevoice.com
www.yourimpossiblevoice.com
twitter.com/YIVJournal

Guidelines:
Your Impossible Voice only accepts submissions through Submittable. Do not email us your submissions or send us hard copies—we will not consider them. We welcome simultaneous submissions, but ask that you withdraw your submission immediately through submittable if accepted elsewhere. We ask that you only submit one piece of prose at a time or three pieces of poetry. We will respond to all submissions, so please be patient. All submissions should be of previously unpublished work. We will not consider work that has appeared elsewhere, whether in print or online. Make sure your name does not appear on the submission itself. We're incredibly serious about this last part.

Your Impossible Voice (ISSN# 2327-381X) is a 501(c)(3) nonprofit published three times a year.

FRIENDS OF YOUR IMPOSSIBLE VOICE

Nancy Ferguson

Stephanie Waite

Bind yourself to us with your impossible voice, your voice! sole soother of this vile despair.
                              -Arthur Rimbaud, "Phrases"

TABLE OF CONTENTS

Sound-Touch

By Laura Legge

Kiki was not fun. She had been forced to live faithfully so her identical twin, Bouba, could survive as her shadow. But a shadow stayed beneath you in sunlight; a shadow wasn't supposed to hover between the sky and the sidewalk, ravening your braids.

Cocaine had stopped Bouba's heart a few nights before, in Seoul, where she had moved a year before to marry Ray Song. That evening she had been in one of her hyperbolic moods, and on the other end of the line Kiki had said, *Shh, shh, baby, heavy your belly with bulgogi*, and Bouba had promised, *Yes, Kikiner, I will*—but of course there was no way to foresee the end of a new and syncopated tune. So now, having survived the restless flight across the Pacific, the hours inside Incheon making mundane arrangements with funeral homes and banks, ordering dreary, unscented bouquets from two-star florists, she was in the front seat of Ray's convertible, wearing a brown corduroy pinafore and a single, utilitarian barrette in her hair, feeling boring as fuck, invisible despite being incarnate, while her twin's memory vogued between them in all its young glory.

Ray was a short, shy powerlifter, and perhaps because of his shyness she already had the sense, three hours into knowing him, that he was more thoughtful than most of the people she encountered. He, for instance, turned down the radio in his car once he learned that Kiki had a form of synesthesia that made her believe each song she heard had a physical form, one that physically touched her, whether it caressed her lips with ghost fingers or slapped her brutally on the back of the skull.

Other than this brief exchange, they talked very little. Kiki was used to that, though she fussed in her head about whether this was making Ray dislike her, or worse, whether this was making him think of other bodies he would rather have in his passenger seat.

He drove to a diner in a neighborhood he called Cheongdam, an American-style eatery that catered to people who felt alien here, but who did not want to make an effort to become less so. He held the car and diner doors for her and chose a table before the hostess could seat them. Across from Kiki, his hair slicked so it could no longer make its own decisions, Ray motored on about the impeccable pancakes, manic about buckwheat and blueberry.

Between the two of them, the Formica seemed to swell. She would never be quiet and comfortable with anyone again. The rest of her life would be spent in affected cafés, saying things that did not need to be said about breakfast food, longing for the ridiculous *songversations* she used to share with Boubear. *Kiki, Kikiner, what does a forest cat say when it loses its fur, Kiki when you're not with me, I says brr brr brr!* Though it made her feel archetypical and embarrassed, Kiki started to cry.

"No, no tears," Ray said. "It's not as tough a choice as I made it sound. You'll get the blueberry."

Kiki knew she was supposed to giggle at that joke. This was what women did in order to be attractive, to crank the confidence of the person they were with. Bouba would have laughed, and she would have found a way not to be demeaned but to be galvanized by that forced music. Yoked as ever to her Kikiness, she said, "I think we should figure out the funeral arrangements."

The server came and filled their mugs with black coffee from a pot in the shape of a boombox. Kiki lifted hers the way a dumbwaiter might, missing the corner of her mouth and trickling that heat down her cheek. She cringed as the liquid touched her skin, not because it was hot but because she had not readied herself to be touched. "Yes," Ray said, drinking his coffee without any spillage. "That's the reason we're here."

The only reason he would be here. She cried more intensely. Her eyes had become her enemies. She told Ray she had a wonderful idea for the funeral, a shimmering, glimmering idea that Bouba would have loved. She poured two cream packets into her coffee and then worried—could he divine her private thoughts from those off-white whirls? Was there a secret language in their design, as in the celestial patterns of tea leaves, that would lay bare the fact that she had tried hard, so hard, to come up with a fitting idea for the funeral, and her brain was just too plain to conceive of anything poetic, or even pleasurable? Because if there were, Ray would be the one to notice. It was oppressive to be around someone so observant.

"That's great," he said. "Do you want to tell me about it?" Kiki did not answer for a while. She was picturing him having sex with her twin. It disgusted her, but there they were, spinning acid jazz, on a daybed, in sunlight, in torn cotton tunics, in rhythm, in rhythm. Back in the diner, she laid her ear down on the Formica, soothing and cold as an unworn headphone. Kiki did not notice the server's mass approach them until Ray had ordered, on her behalf, and the girl was on her way back to the kitchen.

Though it was nearly imperceptible, Jamie Principle's "Your Love" started licking the long route up Kiki's neck with its tongue of sweat, control, privation. The hopelessness of parting, after glistening in someone's arms for hours, and walking into the clinic of an empty home. This song had been an anthem of her teen nights out with Bouba, more than a decade ago, when they both used to dance with dreamy, abstemious heads and sometimes, at most, pin a boy or girl with their lips to the bathroom graffiti. A thought arrived—what if Kiki combed through Bouba's records, and played a tribute set at the club where it happened? She said to Ray, "No, not yet," and used her hand to shield the coffee and cream in her mug.

Ray started to dance to the Jamie Principle song as if it were ear candy, a banger written to the low standards of most people's Friday nights. In his easiness he was suddenly distant from her. The server came to set their plates on the table, and as she did so, she patted Kiki's shoulder in a way Kiki read as consolatory. Her instinct, which as always she managed to ignore, was to shatter the china against the girl's face. Ray said thank you on her behalf. He decked his pancakes with dark agave and then forced into them with the flank of his fork.

He assumed the superior voice of a food critic. "Perfect mouthfeel," he said.

Laughter filled her mouth like vomit. She cut her pancakes into two dozen equal squares and fit them between her teeth one at a time, careful not even to graze her lips. She noticed a stream of agave running down Ray's chin; of course, in order to neaten him, she needed to reach out with her napkin. She did this on instinct, and only considered how prickly the contact made her feel when she saw her reflection in his lightly steamed glasses. But then did it really make her feel prickly, or was she confusing a thought for a sensation? The tail end of "Your Love" was tonguing the inside of her ear—*I can't let go, I can't let go*—and she stroked the sureness of Ray's chin, its permanence in the shadow of this ephemeral song; but then when the tune ended, abashed, she rushed her hand back to her side of the table. It took time to trust sureness. For now, unlike the singer, she found it easier to let go.

Ray told Kiki to come over, so she agreed to come over. She passed out, full of pancakes, on his convertible seat, and only woke up when he blasted an insistent dancehall track, one that spit gobs of Scotch bonnet in her face. Then they walked up to the walk-up together; he had already filled it with blue balloon flowers, luxuriant strings of catmint and silver thyme, a finery of brilliant color that stressed the dullness of Kiki's brown pinafore.

Kiki knew, from the photos Bouba had sent in frenzies every few weeks, between long, sore spells of radio silence that demanded of Kiki great and consistent mercy, that her twin had stored her records in a bathtub lined with purple silk. This was one of the many impulses that had illuminated her charm, and she had been able to indulge it because Ray made enough money to rent a place with a separate shower, and because Kiki had spouted encouragement in *songversation*: *You, you, you there, Bou Bou Boubear, all the dance eyes deep in silk, you make them turn and stare.*

"Can I interest you in some more coffee?" Ray asked now, ramming her polished leather suitcase beside an industrial-sized foot massager, a wedding gift Kiki had chosen at random from across the Pacific, at sea in their Korean-language registry, and which was still confined to its cardboard.

Kiki already felt drugged by the diner's caffeine, but she said yes, because the word had perfect mouthfeel. "I'm just going to use the bathroom first," she added.

Once in the bathroom, Kiki locked the door and knelt before the tub. The bare floor cooled her knees directly through the flaws in her well-worn tights. What kind of a freezing life had her sister lived here, with her devoted husband, without a bathmat, without a felted scrap or flatweave? Had they suffered every time they stepped from the shower and spread water into the grouting, and worse, pressed their soles directly to the bitter tile?

Picturing her sister in this bathroom, shivering, in a wet Seoul winter, remembering her illusion of Bouba and Ray on the daybed— it hit Kiki, pummeled her, that her sister's absence was not a spiritual fact but a physical one. Bouba was somewhere decomposing. They had never been the kind of siblings to embrace, or brush each other's hair, or massage the tensions from one another's traps, although Kiki had watched her sister do these tender things to her infinite friends dozens of times. So what difference did it make to Kiki if Bouba no longer had a body to move around in, when that body had so rarely made contact with hers?

Her hands were shaking. She stabilized them on the records' spines.

Kiki had forced herself to see Bouba perform several times, and what she had noticed was how little the fizzy, heart-first DJ had asked of her audience. She arranged her sets so the audience knew the exact progression their emotions should follow, and having run fluently through that range, they floated from her parties on pink clouds. *Touch your audience as often as you do yourself*, Kiki told herself, as she hunted the stacks for obvious nuance. Sueño Latino went in the Sensual pile, Giorgio Moroder in the Dispassionate, Shabba Ranks in the Aggressive. If she added a slow, introspective jam to the sequence, she followed it with a love song of 128 beats per minute.

The records settled in their separate columns, she removed the silk lining from the tub, inserted the stopper, and turned on the taps. She watched herself in the lightly misted mirror as she undressed, her parts wedded in that haze, no longer riven by veins. When its tideline was high enough, she stepped into the bath and lay down. The water sliced her neck, hands, and feet from her body, and when she rolled and flexed them, it seemed she was doing so through telekinesis. If only she could sink her entire self beneath the surface, maybe she could merge with the water as she had with its mist. She lowered herself far enough to dampen her bottom lip, and then farther, to cast bubbles when she breathed.

Somewhere down the hall, Ray was clanging pans. The sounds were little silver hooks that pierced the back of her neck and lifted her above the steam. She planted her feet on the cold tile, careful not to damage any vinyl.

Bound in a monogrammed towel, *B & R*, Kiki forced her cold feet to walk to the kitchen. Ray was leaning his hips into its marble island, spacing rosemary around a raw pot roast. He looked up and said, "You must be cold. If you want to get comfortable, Bouba's dresser is still full."

To him she was a reptile with an obvious temperature, or worse, a paper doll easily dressed and thus satisfied. Desire and rage entered her bloodstream, and there was no way to anticipate what power they would give her—if only he could see this much, he would understand that she was a living mystery. He would never be able to rheostat her feelings. Kiki moved closer to Ray's ironed denim, to the animal rump he was hunched over. She seamed her side to his and allowed that sudden voltage to thrill her. Because that was the privilege of being alive. Because she had chosen not to pollute her plasma and dance her life force dry and as a result here she was, choosing to touch this strong man.

Her pleasure took a back seat to her hostility. Maybe a physical fact could be a spiritual one, too, because now she was dragging a phantom limb around, one that was the size of a full woman, one that still had a dresser full of playsuits and pullovers and cold-shoulder tops so she could wake up in the spirit-morning and get beautiful. Kiki worked herself into such a fury that she shoved Ray into the marble. Her towel fell. She stood barefoot on the kitchen floor, her nipples screaming from the cold, and she felt quite sure she would rather be dead than be standing here in a body she didn't ask for and could only sometimes control, one that wolfed pancakes, one that wept saltwater, one that stood before other bodies and let them read her temperature and sensations and needs without asking, as if her swollen breasts and slight waist and the boned arch of her eyebrows were not hers and hers alone.

Ray rescued the towel from the ground and wrapped her like a paper doll. "You'll be okay," he promised, and held her tightly. It was hard to tell, in this confused surge of lust and indignation and above all fear, but she believed she was choosing to stay in his arms because it felt good.

This man ate meat and fat and flour in a precise ratio, daily. He channeled his darkness into a barbell and squatted until his muscles were so shredded they had no choice but to heal. He made himself in his own image every day; she did not question his decision to play god. Still enfolding her from behind, the towel keeping her modest from collar to knee, he asked about her funeral plans. It was as if he knew Kiki—though he had only ever known a physical double—because of course the way to calm her from this kind of frenzy was to lock her thoughts on something specific. She achieved focus. And because she had just been so physically bare, it didn't seem any more vulnerable to admit, out loud, "I want to play a set at the club where it happened."

"That's a beautiful idea," he said, sincerely. "Everyone wants to be part of something big. The crowd will love it."

It was embarrassing to have him take her performance seriously, she who wore mock turtlenecks and sensible shoes to clubs, she who danced as incoherently as a pre- sliced magician's assistant and who, as a consequence, rarely tried. She told him, "Keep your expectations low. I'm pretty hard to love."

Ray tightened her already tight towel, making a funerary bouquet of her bones. "That's not true," he said. "I love you like a sister already."

And why was it that every condolence he had offered had fallen on her skin soft as breath, but these words whipped her with a violence the silent body could never muster?

It was a nightmare night—a strangler, armed with a cord of braided hair, lay her down on a monogrammed towel and said, *It hurts worst if you struggle*, only it was Bouba's lost birdsong, *Kikiner, it all feels better as a blur, Kikiner, let the whole world fuzz like fur*—and as Kiki kicked and curved she listened to Ray through the wall, rushing through arrangements with the death-club owner, who seemed desperate to accommodate his wishes. Kiki gathered that she was to replace a girl known as La Physique, who had conveniently come down with laryngitis, which had first silenced her and then milked her energy. When she finally slept, genuinely slept, it was after she heard Ray say, "Trust me, she's just as good."

The next day was so unclouded Kiki had to wear Bouba's sunglasses. Ray insisted on handling the mundane preparations, following up with the florists Kiki had phoned, canceling her tentative plans with funeral homes, lodging the records in laundry bags—she wrote him an itemized list—and while he did so, he threw the car keys at her, and she thought no, but hated the mouthfeel of that word, and she said yes, and imagined Boubear singing something she never had, *Yes, I'll confess, fess, to get it off my chest, chest, Kiki, you're the best, best.*

So she tornadoed through her suitcase and found a romper she had intended only to wear overnight, under covers, and she put it on instead of her pinafore. She left her legs nude and played the crunchiest, hair-pulling-est R&B she could find on Ray's satellite radio, and she silenced the automaton who was telling her where to drive and flew the convertible through a series of potential wrong turns. Here she was, wind-blown, sensational, in the opening credits of a film that had her name listed first.

Kiki came to earth again in Myeongdong, where she ordered too many pork cutlets and downed them anyway, and, fortified by all that iron, bought compacts of crystal prisms that she layered on her high cheeks. Here, though bodied, she was invisible. So when she felt the urge to that afternoon, she danced, she ran, she bought a dress of blue velvet, she broke in a pair of men's brogues, she slopped coffee into her mouth until her heart beat beyond her control, she whistled, she rested her palms in her armpits, on her breasts, she chose for a few hours not to struggle against what she wanted to do.

Then, in the gloaming, she drove to Ray's walk-up. She idled outside and honked for him; her legs were comfortable on the car seat, so she didn't force them to move. She had changed into the velvet dress and the brogues, and as she glanced down she thought, I have hips. When Ray came out in an oversized tuxedo, struggling with the awkward weight of the two record-filled laundry bags, she did not crave a compliment from him. Still, he said, "Kiki, you're champagne."

She found the club without Ray or the robot; when she opened the double glass doors, while Ray balanced both laundry bags on his muscular thigh, she revealed a world of few details. Everything inside the club was made of teal-tinted glass, the bar, the booth, the dance floor, the ceiling, the cages in which paid women were showing their power to bend. Plain and blue, the room was a body of water. Kiki stood in the middle and posed like a memorial statue in a public fountain, her velvet shining, her figure patently suited to its surroundings.

Satisfied that enough early-comers had seen her statue-self, she moved to the booth. She hummed as she slipped each record from its sleeve and into a cenotaph for Bouba; as she did, Cherelle licked the alcove behind her ear, Ornette Coleman traced a finger down the front of her velvet. After half an hour the monument reached eye level, and when Kiki could no longer see the crowd that was forming, she stopped building. She would spin each record from top to bottom, the structure gradually depressing, until finally she would be standing behind its foundation, unprotected, and that is when she would lift the microphone reserved only for abrasive soca horns and *Get your hands up, put that ass up*, and say, in front of all these night creatures with their monstrous pupils, "Sleep sound, Boubear."

Enough people had arrived; she cut the canned music in favor of her first single of the night, Frankie Knuckles x Chaka Khan, "Ain't Nobody." Over the cenotaph, she glimpsed Ray facing the bar. She had been so mighty an hour earlier, repelled by his overlong sleeves, inflated by an afternoon of sun and whim and performance, and now that he had removed his absurd jacket and turned his back, she felt a sudden, imperious need for him to notice her.

Then came Chaka's voice, a phantom in the house of glass. *Ain't nobody/loves me better.* A question scratched at Kiki's chest—what had Ray and Bouba done and what sensations had they felt while listening to this propulsive bassline? She was about to dip, drop, catwalk, catch the club's attention with her hasty angles, when a column of curls and lipstick came to request a song from her. Each woman in the club was an analogy, an echo of another body in rouge and leather several feet away. In this brine, she lost sight of Ray. Infuriating, having her talent questioned this early in the night, and by someone so replaceable. Kiki pretended to listen to the request, and then she spun Vangelis, "Blush Response."

This song was a plastic mallet, hitting her vertebrae individually, turning each one a different shade of ice, from Alice blue to tea rose. The ice calmed her from this contact, until she spotted Ray again, a drink now in his hand, dancing close to a girl with durian hair. Suddenly the quality of the song changed; it was lighting Kiki's vertebrae in saturated, vicious colors. From above, the club's lasers drilled into her, and the crystal powder on her face, which had for a moment felt no different than her own skin, started to melt, filling her mouth with the sting of ammonia.

She snatched the needle from the record. The room went silent, forcing Ray and the tropical fruit to stop dancing. This power made her feel cohesive again, as she had in the steam, or in the statue pose, and she knew such a cohesive being did not live for anyone's approval. That was when she noticed all the eyes splitting her down her fault lines. Why had Kiki chosen this velvet dress? It cut into her shoulders so deeply it made her arms look plastic. Boiling, bared, she fingered its low bust and forgot to play the next record.

Words came rushing at her, ones she heard most often in Sensual songs, only this crowd had exorcised from them the spirit of love. Each person had decided what song they wanted to hear, and when, and how loudly, and they conceived of these not as preferences but as needs. Worse, they believed Kiki was there to serve them a good time, the way a waitress serves pancakes, and that if they went home to their narcissus pool and cast into it a murky look, or disturbed its surface with tears, that was a failure on Kiki's part.

She was an emptied-out club, so hollow her thoughts echoed inside of her. She understood suddenly why everyone around her was indiscriminate with how they chose to be filled.

Swayed by their demands, Kiki put on Janet Jackson, "Control." When the durian-headed girl started dancing again, grinding a model with silver hair and country teeth, Kiki realized she had at no point been with Ray. She spotted him at the far end of the bar, tapping his too-big dress shoe as the song oscillated from pissed to poised. The figures in the room had loosened, had relearned their limbs, had started to lunge at one another in the animal skin of aggression.

Next Kiki spun "Iceblink," a cheek-peck of techno from Ken Ishii. This song seized Ray. It must have scored a particular episode between him and Bouba, because he did something bizarre and hush-hush, leaned against a high pillar with generous give in his knees and knocked his powerlifter bubble against the glass. It was a strange move. And yet she recognized in it her afternoon in Myeongdong, how right it felt to run sometimes, and stretch, and wedge your hands in your warm armpits, how that polychrome of motion could pull the darkness from you.

For the next few hours, time followed Kiki's metronome. Ray drifted in and out of her sightline, but she only noticed his absence between songs, and even then, she did not assign any emotion to this simple act of noticing. All that mattered was her set had started to win the crowd. They were dancing to what she was spinning, with joy and abandon, and together, Kiki and Kikrowd were creating a world of their choosing. Inside her chest was a disco ball, and a strobe light, and random bursts of confetti—she was no longer an emptied-out club, but a full one, so very full, the kind she imagined Bouba had always chased.

The last oil-brick in her monument was Prince, "The Beautiful Ones." And for once, Kiki's timing was perfect, not too early, as to every party, or too late, as to her sister's rescue. Because right then, someone flipped on the big, fear-of-god lights, and she was left standing in that honest light. The club was half empty already, and those who had stayed scattered to the room's opposite shores. Kiki lifted the microphone from its cradle, just as she had intended to do, and when the microphone was near her lips and she had the power to say *Sleep sound, Boubear*, she heard herself singing along instead. She had once burned through this track at karaoke, but in a mock voice, armored by irony. And now her voice was pretty and cracking, and most of all, hers. The song had grown two arms and was wrapping her from behind, as Ray had with the towel, only these arms were immortal, made of pure light. In the spoken word part she walked off the stage and to the pillar, where Ray was still leaning. By now she was in tears. Her eyes were not her enemies; she could not control the saltwater, but it had reason to fall.

She used Ray's hands to dry her face. Not because she was unable to use her own, but because she didn't have to. He was warm, and now she was, too. Even after the song finished, and she was left standing under harsh lights, having sung her lungs to the point of inflammation, she did not push him away.

Bouba had taken Kiki to see Prince when they were teenagers, virginal, in retainers and rain jackets. In that room, minimal as this one, Bouba first experienced that strange sensation of sound-touch. Prince played a dark chord on the synth and it vibrated until Kiki felt a set of arms cloak her, long and silky, and tighten until she was completely held. At first she convinced herself they belonged to Bouba. But when the song finished and the arms dissolved, her body felt immaculate, and it mattered less where that feeling came from than where it would carry her next.

About the Author

Laura Legge lives and writes in Toronto. She received her MFA from New York University this year. Her writing has most recently appeared in *Mid-American Review*, *Witness*, *Newfound Journal*, *The Walrus*, and *Meridian*, and is upcoming in *North American Review*, *Chicago Quarterly Review*, and *The Capilano Review*. She volunteers in a women's prison and is passionate about criminal justice reform.

Before Roe

By Debby Bloch

Still on my back. Legs spread. Feet held in metal stirrups. I say to Dr. Dubrovnick, whose face peers at me from between my knees, "I can't go through with this."

"Debby," he answers, "it's against the law."

"Please, please. What if this is going to drive me insane?" I feel as if I might indeed go insane.

"There's nothing I can do but make sure you're healthy, whether you continue your pregnancy or whatever you decide or do—if you go somewhere else," Dubrovnick says.

"Where else can I go?" I feel a moment of hope. Maybe he's hinting at some solution he will reveal only if I ask the right question. After all, he's been my OB/GYN for years. He's delivered both my children, been sympathetic about my divorce. I pull my feet from the stirrups and sit up.

He stands and smooths non-existent creases from his long white coat. "Debby, not only can't I refer you to anyone else, I really don't even know anyone else." Dubrovnick pats me on the shoulder.

The disgrace of it all. And the kids. My ex-husband-to-be has already threatened to get custody. If only the divorce were final… If I have this baby, Bruce and Seth are old enough to figure out that something is wrong and young enough to be traumatized by what they figure out.

"My ex will take the children, and the children will find out about me. I can't lose my children." Saying aloud what I've been thinking brings on the sobs that I've suppressed. "What should I do? You've got to help me."

Dubrovnick is silent.

"What if this happened to someone in your family, someone you love?" I ask him.

"I'm afraid I would be in the same position you are."

I can't stop crying. This is no ploy for sympathy although if sympathy gets me a way out, I'll gladly take it.

"Debby, I wish I could help you. My hands are tied on this. You'll have to find your own way. I know, I know." With each "I know" Dubrovnick pats my shoulder. "Take your time." He hands me some tissues. "Don't leave until you feel ready." And just like that, he's gone.

For a certain generation of adults, those were the glory years of sexual freedom, the years after the FDA approved The Pill and before the shock wave of HIV/AIDS hit the world. But it didn't begin that way for me.

It's 1968, I live with my two kids in a two-story house, on a quiet street, in a middle-class neighborhood in Queens, I'm a high school English teacher. My ex has a good job in real estate. That's how it's supposed to be except for one thing. The "marriage-until-death-do-us-part" part has ended in a bitter separation, soon to be a divorce.

But the divorce is the least of my problems. I feel a knot grow in my stomach, a knot with no beginning and no bitter end, no loose string that can help untangle it. It's the worst possible moment in my life to be pregnant. How did I get myself into this fix? Joel. Joel isn't even someone I care about.

This is the punishment my mother warned me about all my life. This pregnancy—this punishment—comes directly from her oldest admonitions. After all, like all good Jewish girls raised in the fifties, I was inculcated with the notion that any excess, any satisfaction of desire, could lead to disaster. Eat an éclair, get ptomaine poisoning and die. Swim before summer's official start—July fourth—get pneumonia and die. Stay out after eleven in the evening, meet a sex maniac, be raped and die. My mother was right. I strayed, I slept with—no, I want to be honest, I fucked—a lot of men, and now I was paying. I laughed at my mother when I was a kid, but now ... But now—sex—I wasn't doing anything different from everyone else I knew. Like them, I supported the Civil Rights Movement. Marched against the war in Vietnam. Sure—make love, not war. Look where it got me.

It began simply enough when Renée and I decided to go to a club not far from where we both lived. We laughed as we left my kids with the babysitter. Two high school teachers out for a big night. In Queens. But it was always fun to go with Renée. Not only were we confidantes since what felt like our simultaneous divorces, but our complementary appearances acted like magnets. Renée had dark hair and a lean, fashionable figure, while I was somewhat rounder with strawberry blonde hair and the fair skin of a natural redhead. Maybe we'd meet someone, maybe hang out, have a drink or two.

In the club, there was a long bar with a red leather edge, a few small tables with black, reflective tops and, around the tables, small metal chairs with round red leather seats. All empty. There were probably around thirty, forty people leaning on the bar but facing into the room, standing around, walking around the room, eying each other. It was too early in the evening for people to have paired off.

There was a combo playing a mix of popular songs of the past couple of years, "Light My Fire," "Cherish," "Can't Take My Eyes Off You." That's the beginning. The beginning I wish I could erase. The moment when I realized the drummer was looking at me, smiling. When he saw I noticed him, he raised one stick and with the other hand brushed the cymbals— swoosh, swoosh, schwing. A kind of musical pick-up line. I smiled back and made some sort of flirty movement with my hair.

I don't remember anything we said. Of course I do remember leaving the bar with Joel and going to his apartment nearby, a small apartment on the second floor of a brick building. As the elevator door opened, I smelled the familiar apartment-house-hall blend of cooked onions and brewed coffee. His door had the usual two locks, one deadbolt supplied by the building and one lock he had installed, the kind that couldn't be jimmied or opened with a master key. The all-purpose living/eating room was just like the ones I'd seen in other single men's apartments—a semi-broken-down sofa, probably salvaged from his marriage or his mother, two chrome and vinyl chairs at a small, round Formica table with the remnants of supper, or lunch, or the previous night's meal. He led me into the bedroom. A double mattress and box spring sat on the floor. Joel hurriedly smoothed out the sheets and blanket.

Talk about being blind. I'd never used a diaphragm in my marriage and I don't know why I didn't figure out I needed one now. The Pill had been on the market for a while, but even that news passed me by. I expected him to use a condom, but he said, "I don't like how condoms feel. Don't worry, I'll pull out."

By the time he said, "I'll pull out," I was really hot. I wanted him at least as much as he wanted me. After that year of rejection, the year in which my marriage fell apart, being wanted was all the aphrodisiac I needed. Joel was cute. Maybe "cute" made him seem less threatening. He was about five foot eight—a good difference from my five feet three inches—slender, but with well-developed arm muscles. Probably the drumming.

Joel was in no hurry to get to the ending. He sucked on my fingers. That was an incredibly sexy feeling. He was a good kisser, as we said in high school. Lingering. Slow. Lingering and slow all over my body. And then he entered, and he did pull out. But clearly not soon enough.

A few weeks later, I felt my breasts grow tender. My nipples swelled and the pressure of my bra made them hurt. Then I realized that more than a month had gone by without my period.

I am pregnant and I am desperate, desperate in the true sense of the word, without hope. I ask my closest friends if they know of anyone, a person, a hospital, anywhere in the country, where I can go to terminate the pregnancy. Nothing. I ask my friends to ask their friends, but everyone knows pretty much the same people. None of those people are of any use. And asking Joel for help is out of the question. I saw him only once after that night. We met for coffee and realized that one night together had been enough for both of us. I'm not even sure I can remember how to find him. Besides I don't want anything from him. The brief romance, if you could call it that, is over, dead, but what we started together is not.

I think of a friend in New Jersey, Betty, a friend I haven't seen since a year or two after college. Maybe Betty or her lawyer husband will know the right kind of doctor. Or other kind of person. It's not that I think Betty is any different from my current friends, but we New Yorkers always think of New Jersey as somewhat disreputable, the homeland of gangsters. I imagine the small cities and placid suburbs of Jersey as a kind of *terra incognita*. As it turns out, Betty does remember a hospital in Newark that is supposed to cater to "female problems," but when I call information for the hospital number, it's disconnected.

Then, unexpectedly, Eileen, a teacher in the math department at school, comes up to me in the cafeteria.

She sits down next to me and speaks so softly I can barely hear her. "I understand you have a problem. I might be able to help you. Can you meet me after school? I'm parked right outside, a black Ford Mustang."

"Sure," I say. Eileen isn't even a friend, just another teacher in the huge high school of thirty-five hundred kids. I'm surprised that Eileen has even heard about me. I'm surprised that there's a chance that Eileen could be the one to help me. I'm even surprised that Eileen has a Mustang, a car for a younger person.

"I hear you have a problem, not a school problem," Eileen begins once we're in her car.

"Yes, I do." I don't care how Eileen learned about the pregnancy.

"Do you want some advice?"

My scalp gets tight. I feel the individual hairs rise. The last thing I need is some do-gooder telling me what to do. I say nothing, just nod.

"I have some experience with this problem—not my own—but someone very close to me. You'll understand why I don't want to say who."

I nod again.

"Can you get your hands on some money? You'll need twelve hundred dollars in cash plus money for airfare, a hotel room for a few nights, food, taxis," Eileen says.

"Airfare to where?" I ask.

"San Juan."

"As in Puerto Rico?"

"Yes."

"I can get the money together." It's a lot of money, but I figure I can somehow make it work with a combination of a small savings account and credit cards. "Can you give me the name or address there?" I begin to reach into my bag for a pen.

"You won't need a pen. You'll remember the details I'm going to tell you. When you get to San Juan, get a taxi at the airport. Tell the driver you want a 'guesthouse' and a 'woman's doctor.'"

"I don't speak Spanish."

"You don't need Spanish. Believe me, the driver will understand. He'll take you to a small hotel. It will be a modest guesthouse, nothing more elaborate. Ask him to wait. Register, drop your bag, and get back in the taxi. He'll be waiting. Then he'll take you to the place you need and he will tell you the fare is two hundred dollars. Pay him. Twenties are good."

"How do I know this will work?" I ask.

"You don't," Eileen answers.

"How do I know I'll be in the right taxi?"

"You have to hope that you are. I guess you could look for a different taxi if the driver doesn't know what you're talking about."

"Will the person, you know—I mean not the driver, the other person—be a doctor or at least a nurse?" I ask.

"I don't know," Eileen answers.

"Will it be a clean place?"

"I don't know."

"I could be—be killed." Immediately, a word jumps into my mind, flashes before my eyes in bold letters: ***butchered***. ***Butchered*** is the word that always appears in the news stories about illegal abortions, and all abortions are illegal.

"You won't know any of this ahead of time. My heart really goes out to you, my dear, but if this is what you have to do, it's the only plan I know of."

"And the person you know, the person who did this?" I ask.

"She's fine."

I arrange for my mother to take care of Bruce and Seth, concocting a story about a teachers' conference: "Teaching Shakespeare" in Stratford, Ontario. I'm sure my mother thinks I'm running off with some man, but I let her believe that.

I don't think at all about the cells growing within me as a life. Of course I know about embryonic and fetal development from high school bio books. But those are not the pictures that come to mind. Instead I picture lurid headlines in the *Daily News* as if there is a movie running behind my eyes. "Teacher's Terror: Back Alley Abortion." "No Can Do: Knitting Needles Botch Abortion." "Queens Mother Bleeds Out in Emergency Room." And the photos. Is that my sheet-draped corpse next to the rather good photo of me at a picnic? Are those my children clinging to their grandmother in the funeral parlor? Is that Renée, covering her face, as she arrives at the cemetery?

I pack a small bag and board the Eastern Airlines flight from JFK airport to San Juan. I leave New York in a fine misty rain. I arrive in Puerto Rico, and I feel the wall of hot, humid, tropical air hit me as soon as I walk out of the plane. I remember that particular smell of tropical air from a family vacation my ex and I took with the kids long before our divorce was on the horizon. I make my way through the airport, following the signs in English and Spanish to the taxi stand. Which is the magic taxi? Which one has the right driver? Should I go to the rank of taxis lined up at the stand or choose one of the people hanging around saying, "Taxi, lady" and grabbing at my small suitcase? I go to the first taxi in line.

I lean forward as the driver puts the car in gear. "I need a guesthouse and a woman's doctor," I say.

"Okay," the driver answers.

I have no idea of what *okay* means. Does he understand me at all? I can do nothing but wait.

We drive from the airport, through the outskirts of San Juan, into the middle of the city and then to a tree-lined block of medium-sized houses. The driver pulls up in front of a white clapboard house, two stories, green trim. It looks welcoming enough with its covered porch shading a few chairs.

The driver and I get out of the cab, and he takes my bag from my hand. A knock on the door is answered by an ample middle-aged woman, her graying hair held back in a bun. I cannot understand what the driver says to the woman or what she replies, but then the woman turns to me.

"*¡Pase! ¡Adelante!*" the woman says. "*Pase por aquí, por favor,*" and she gestures to me to follow her up a flight of stairs.

I take a deep breath and follow her.

"*Este es su cuarto.*"

As the woman opens the door, I find myself ushered into a pleasant if old-fashioned room. It is painted a pale yellow. There is a wicker chair with a flowered yellow cushion and a double bed with a white chenille spread and a metal headboard painted white.

"*Aquí está su baño.*" The woman points to a door that leads to a private bath. I'm almost ready to breathe a sigh of relief when I realize that this is only the first stop. I follow the woman down the stairs, sign the register, and get back into the cab.

The cab continues through the streets of Puerto Rico. We aren't in the bustling heart of San Juan. I don't know where we are. The driver pulls up in front of a narrow gray building and points to the long flight of wooden stairs that leads to its front door.

"Two hundred dollars," he says.

I pay him and realize that in all our time together—probably close to two hours—he has said exactly four words to me: "okay" and "two hundred dollars."

I get out of the cab and walk up the stairs. There is no sign as to whether this is an office, a private house, or a deserted building. I look for a bell or buzzer and seeing none, I knock. There is no answer. I try the door, which opens easily. I'm in a small vestibule. The walls of the narrow hall are a dingy beige and the floor is brown, worn linoleum. At the end of the hall, behind a desk, sits a wizened old man.

"*¿Si? ¿Que?*" And then "Yes?" he asks.

"I need help from a woman's doctor," I say.

"What kind of help?" he asks. His Spanish accent does not affect his perfect English and no expression changes his somber face. His face is thin, angular. It seems etched from some ancient stone.

"I'm," I hesitate, "pregnant, and …" I can't go on.

"Yes, what is it you want?" Now he sounds impatient.

"I cannot have this baby because …"

He cuts me off. "I know what you want. You want an operation. You want us to take the baby away from inside you. You know that is against the law. You cannot behave like a … like a …" He seems to be searching for some English word. "You cannot do as you wish with a man and then expect someone else to take care of your problems. What you want is a terrible thing. It may help you, but it will destroy another. You will go to hell and that unborn soul will have no chance to find God's way. You know this is a Catholic country and that what you are asking is against God's laws too."

I actually feel the blood leave my face and brain. I think I will faint or throw up, but I don't know whether the nausea is from my pregnancy, from the Puerto Rican heat, from the dark room, or from the old man's words. I do not know what to say, anything to stop the conversation. Am I going to be arrested? Here? In Puerto Rico? I want to flee but have that nightmare feeling of being rooted to the spot.

Then the old man continues. "We are taking a chance to help you, a very big chance, with the government and with God. That will be one thousand dollars."

I reach into my handbag for the envelope filled with twenty-dollar bills. The old man takes it from me with palsied hands. He removes the bills from the envelope and places them in a neat pile on the ancient desk in front of him. Slowly he counts each bill, his hands shaking as he moves the bill from the uncounted pile to the pile he has counted.

"Come back tomorrow morning. Eight o'clock. Take this card. Do not eat anything."

I don't know whether I have lost a thousand dollars to a scam artist or whether I have voluntarily given up a thousand dollars meant for someone who might have helped me, because I do know that I will not go back to that old, gray man and his shaking hands. But then, that last sentence he said seems reassuring. "Do not eat anything." That is the kind of thing a doctor would say. I walk slowly down the steep stairs to the street and look back at the building and then at the card. The card has the address of the building, only that and nothing more. The same cab, same driver wait for me at the curb.

I don't sleep that night. I play and replay the scene with the old man. At times his shaking hands seem larger than life. At times, it is his voice that I keep hearing. More than once, I throw off the covers and sit up, planning to pack my bag and leave, but each time, I lie back again. When I'm not thinking of the old man, I think of the moment when I met Joel. I keep hoping I can somehow wind the film backward and avoid everything that followed.

The next morning, I step outside the guesthouse to find a taxi waiting. I realize that I don't need the card. Again the same driver. The cab pulls up in front of the familiar gray building and again I mount the narrow stairs. This time my tentative knock on the door is answered. A woman in a white nurse's uniform opens the door.

"*¡Buen dia!*" she says.

When I answer "good morning," the nurse switches to English. "Are you the young woman who was here yesterday afternoon?"

I nod.

"Come into this room."

The room into which I'm ushered seems to come from a different world than the narrow, dusty vestibule. It is like the doctors' dressing rooms with which I'm familiar, white paint, a small bench, a locker with no lock, a curtain.

I follow the nurse's instructions to undress and put on a gown. I step out of the dressing room, and the nurse is there, waiting. She leads me into what appears to be an operating room. There is a high table with stirrups at one end. Above the table is a large light, the kind that can be maneuvered into its needed position. There is another table, a small one, with instruments on a white towel. I feel reassured, somewhat, but still … This all appears ordinary. Yet it seems bizarre after my encounters with the mysterious taxi driver and the old man.

A white-gowned man strides into the room. "Good morning. I am Doctor Diaz. I think you met my father yesterday. Today, I am going to give you some anesthesia. You won't feel any pain, and then I will remove the tissue that's bothering you, the tissue from your uterus. You will sleep a little afterwards, and my nurse will watch you. When you wake up, you will be fine. You may have a little spotting. For that eventuality, we will give you some pads. Are you flying back to the mainland tonight?"

"Tomorrow," I whisper.

"That's better," he says and helps me onto the operating table.

Some time later, I'm not sure exactly how much time, the nurse helps me into the taxi. Back in my hotel room, I pull the white chenille spread off the bed, slide under the covers, and sleep all that afternoon and evening.

I don't feel anything except very tired until I am on the plane the next day. Then the cramping begins. It is mild at first but then grows stronger. I don't know how I can make it through the flight. Should I tell the stewardess? What should I tell the stewardess? I can hear the PA announcement: "Is there a doctor aboard the plane? We have a woman bleeding out from an abortion." No one will come to my help. I don't even know if I am bleeding and I'm afraid to go to the restroom to find out. What if blood runs down my legs for everyone to see? Perhaps this is an infection. After all, I don't really know who this Dr. Diaz is. Maybe the old man did the operation while I was knocked out by ether.

"Please God," I pray under my breath, "don't delay this plane. Please God, don't let me die." Over and over I say the same words until they become simply, "Please God. Please God. Please God."

If I live, I don't know how I will make it home from the airport. At least Renée will be meeting me. I won't have to deal with any more taxis.

In the airport, Renée takes one look at my white face and doubled-over body and says, "You're going to the emergency room."

"Call Dubrovnick," I say. "And call my mother. Tell her food poisoning. She'll believe that since she always thinks we'll get poisoned if we eat anything but her cooking."

Dubrovnick meets me in the Emergency Room, examines me, instructs a nurse to take me into a small operating room, and then— nothing—until he reappears as I awaken.

"Don't worry," he says. "You are clean. I don't know where you went—and I don't want to know—but whoever it was knew what he was doing. You have no infection. There was a bit more placental tissue left and that was the cause of your cramping. I removed it and now you'll be fine. You are one lucky girl." He pats my shoulder once again.

"Thanks," I murmur, and as I fall asleep again, I think "for nothing."

"Before Roe" appears in a slightly different form in Debby Bloch's novel, *That Old Song and Dance*

About the Author

Debby Bloch's first novel, *That Old Song and Dance*, was published by Barbarian Books. Her short works have appeared in *Able Muse* and *Switchback*. A retired professor from both the University of San Francisco and the City University of New York, she is the author of seven books and numerous articles related to her academic field. Debby has a BA in English from Brooklyn College, an MS in counseling from St. John's University and a PhD in organizational studies from New York University. In 2009 she graduated from the University of San Francisco's MFA in writing program. Debby lives in San Francisco and Ashland with her husband and reader extraordinaire, Martin.

[misread graffiti]

By Laura Post

I have bursts of being a body, but they never last long.

I buried a lightbulb,
thought it might hatch fire,
set those lazy fields ablaze.

We unshelve
ourselves sometimes, dog-eared
and plaintive—spells of them tucked away
for once of us.

Our neighbors keep us up at night
firing
                    BBs
   at an old mattress :

that we
                    had control over our dreams.

Response to Bhanu Kapil

1. Who are you and whom do you love?

I pulled my teeth out
one by
        one,
felt the blood run sticky down my chin like
watermelon juice,
held my smile in the palm of my hand.

2. Where did you come from/how did you arrive?

I come from a blue line ballpoint-carved into a table,
the same self and a line of unremembered bodies.

I arrived of love contorted by suffering.

I was a key cut loose before the storm rolled in.

3. How will you begin?

I read somewhere that every drop of seawater
holds one billion atoms of gold:
Let me cry about something stupid.

4. How will you live now?

I will be the night sky,
my every star a green light.

5. What is the shape of your body?

Pack yourself in two boxes:

Loneliness and
oneliness.

6. Who is responsible for the suffering of your mother?

My mother was the one who showed me
how to burn holes with a magnifying glass
by letting the sun funnel through.

7. What do you remember about the earth?

My brother and I used to grow alligators
in the bathroom sink,

angry green capsules that bloomed
into spongyslick reptiles.

They slid through our grubby fingers
when we squoze.

8. What are the consequences of silence?

I was nothing but the tamarack's shaking throat.
He wrote: "You display more emotion in your eyes than I display in my
    entire body."
Only alarm would cure my hiccups.

9. Tell me what you know about dismemberment.

My mother likes to rearrange furniture that she brings home from the
    curb.
She is a woman with no questions.

10. Describe a morning you woke without fear.

I was the soil, mouth full of insects.

11. How will you/have you prepare(d) for your death?

As a child I would pour grape juice into a plastic cup
and leave it to the thirsty July air.

12. And what would you say if you could?

Be patient with me.

The questions in this poem were originally written and asked by Bhanu Kapil in her book, *The Vertical Interrogation of Strangers*, published by Kelsey St. Press.

About the Author

Laura Post is from New Jersey and currently lives in Ohio. Her poetry has appeared in *The Moth Magazine*, *New South*, *Occupy Poetry*, and elsewhere.

The Eating Contest

By Timothy DeLizza

Surrealist sexual playing cards lined the wall of Dali's restaurant. Each was as small as a regular playing card and had the pair making love to each other in unlikely positions. Some cards had two men, some two women, some a woman with a monster. Often one or both of the lovers were blindfolded and innocent-looking—almost unaware as to what was happening to their lower body—but smiling just enough for the viewer to know that they were pleased by what was happening.

A platform where bands typically played was transformed into a place for the Law Association Awards. All of the major New York firms had tables. Sitting around Raul Dangler's table were six partners and four other summer associates from Harper & Mann LLP. Lorraina Merewether, the head of the firm's environmental practice, smiled seductively at the head of the table.

The first course was foie gras mini-hamburgers served with lychee martinis.

After this, an award was given to Harper & Mann LLP for being the most environmentally friendly firm for its use of solar power in its San Francisco Office, and for its revolutionary program moving from paper paychecks to electronic paychecks. As the award was given, Ms. Merewether gestured for the waiter. The waiter put a warm piece of walnut cranberry bread next to her arm.

The second course was pangolin steak and mustard-crusted raw salmon served with fresh raspberries in sake.

Another firm won an award for workplace diversity.

The third course was a half lobster served with a red wine from California.

Other firms won awards for promoting women in the workplace.

The fourth course was a tin tree sculpture with cheesecake lollipops growing from its branches. The lollipop tree was served with cotton candy flavored whipped cream on the side. At the base of the tree was a rectangular glass case of living Japanese beetles covered with a viscous golden fluid. Throughout the course, hidden jet streams beneath the glass case shot new fluids, causing the beetles to change colors to deep red, purple, and finally black. The wings of the beetles made a metallic but soothing sound as they scraped against each other. With each new liquid the pitch changed.

Between the fourth and fifth courses, Harper & Mann received a Women's Rights award for its pro bono program for battered women. Ms. Merewether was also awarded individually for her leadership within that program. As she accepted the award, the announcer asked her how she did it. "Thankfully, I don't need much sleep," Ms. Merewether said. The crowd laughed.

The fifth course was deep-sea bass served still sizzling on a rock.

The final course was the largest cheesecake Raul had ever seen, crusted with candied Japanese Beetles.

"I can't eat more," said a fellow summer associate at the edge of the table.

"Are you kidding? I can finish that myself," Raul said.

"A hundred dollars says you can't," Ms. Merewether said.

"You're on," Raul said.

Ms. Merewether tapped the chest of the waiter, as if they were old friends. "Has anyone ever finished one of these alone?"

"Not in my three years here."

"Okay Raul. If you finish it, a hundred bucks. But you throw up—you lose," Ms. Merewether said.

"I can do this," Raul said.

Raul asked for an oversized spoon so he could eat the cheesecake in fewer bites. Each time he plunged the spoon in, the candied beetles' shells would give resistance, then crackle and let the spoon plunge into the buttery soft insides of the cake. About halfway through, another partner put two fifty-dollar bills on the table. "Stop now, I'll pay. You're going to kill yourself."

"No! I'm okay. I'm okay. I can do this," Raul said.

"I don't think you can do this," the partner said.

"No, he's a big boy—he agreed to do it. Let him do it. A deal's a deal," said Ms. Merewether. "Raul, you can stop any time."

"I'm okay. I can do this," Raul said and lifted his oversized spoon again.

Dali's manager came over. "If he finishes it—Dali's will put his picture up right there …" the manager said. Behind Raul was an empty frame between two playing cards with olive skinned women and monsters. "A photo of a Cameron Diaz was there—but someone stole it earlier this week."

"Eat! Eat! Eat!" said the table when he resumed.

The kitchen help and table-bussers trickled in around the room, smiling to each other and speaking inaudibly among themselves. One started clapping but it did not catch.

Two bites before the cheesecake was finished, regret flooded Raul's face. He fled to the bathroom. When he returned, the entire table clapped, the tables nearby hooted and howled. The manager took photos as he sat and finished the final bites. The kitchen staff drifted back to their jobs and the other tables returned to their own conversations.

"Would you like to take the pangolin blood home with you?" the waiter asked. "It helps settle the stomach."

"Raul, do you want to bring home pangolin blood?" Ms. Merewether asked. Without waiting for a response, she patted the bill. The waiter took the bill away.

Ms. Merewether and Raul shared a cab to the after-party.

"What asshole becomes a cab driver without knowing how to get to 250 Fifth Avenue? It's part of a fucking grid," Ms. Merewether said loud enough for the taxi driver to hear. "How is your stomach?"

"Completely fine. I could've made it if I didn't eat Joanna's lobster," Raul said.

"You ate Joanna's entire lobster?" Ms. Merewether asked.

Raul smiled proudly.

The cab took them to the after-party, which was on a bar at the top of a midtown highrise. The bar was full of plush purple couches, and ambient music floated through the air. When they walked in, two Harper & Mann summer associates were already out on the balcony with shot glasses full of neon fluid. The rain had paused and they, laughing, tossed their shot glasses over the balcony edge onto the city streets below.

"Honey, come with me," Ms. Merewether said to Raul, who watched the summers from the inside portion of the bar. "You did good tonight. You deserve something."

Ms. Merewether led Raul to an old wooden door, which then opened to a large room. Half the walls were windows that looked over the Manhattan skyline. In the dead center was the Empire State Building. The view gave Raul a sense of power. Lining the walls were small cages filled with spiders.

Ms. Merewether was already in one of the reddish-brown leather couches drinking a clear liquid filled with ice and cucumbers. She looked over the skyline.

"Lie down. They're getting us cigars. Take off your shirt."

"My shirt?"

Ms. Merewether's smile reminded Raul of the nude women on the playing cards. Raul rested in the nearest couch and removed his shirt. He took pride that his body remained muscular and toned with only two days in the gym a week this summer. An attractive woman came with one of the smaller cages and laid the cage on his chest.

"What the hell is that?" Raul asked.

"Just let the spider bite you. It's fucking amazing. Fucking amazing."

Raul's concerned face melted into a smile. "Okay, I'm game."

"Good. This is going to be good," Ms. Merewether said. She held down one of Raul's arms while the matron held down the other.

The spider was bright leathery yellow with light green splotches. It was the size of a baseball. Once out of the cage, the spider crawled across Raul's skin. Raul's body jerked instinctually. The spider's feet felt like glass pins.

"Don't worry, it's coming. If it hits a vein—that's payday."

The spider bit Raul's chest. Numbness flooded his body and everything seemed well.

Before the matron could recapture it, the spider scurried along his arm and bit down a second time on his wrist. Raul screamed and would have crushed the spider if his arm was not pinned. Looking down he saw a sack of eggs pulsating in the veiny part of his wrist.

Ms. Merewether laughed.

"Leave them, leave them," the matron said. "Wait." She recaptured the spider and left the room quickly.

"These places have to smuggle Tsche spider eggs into the country on the backs of carriers," Ms. Merewether whispered, "which is both expensive and dangerous—especially if you have a premature hatching. Those are fucking valuable."

Another woman brought cucumber drinks to them while they waited. The drink tasted like sticky, lightly sweetened water, but Raul sensed it was heavily alcoholic.

An elderly Asian man entered. "I'll give you $20,000 if you let them hatch," he said. His voice was calm and smoky.

"I can do that," Raul said, laughing. "Can I still drink while I wait?"

The old Asian man smiled. "Only expensive drinks—it gives the spider's bite extra flavor. You come here and the drinks are free." The beautiful woman returned and began wrapping a soft white cloth around Raul's wrist.

"Here here," Raul said.

His wrist was turning purple and the bandages around it red with blood. Like this, they returned to the larger group outside.

Raul sat on a fluffy couch between Ms. Merewether and a fellow summer associate. As soon as Raul sat he started laughing uncontrollably. When this subsided, he turned to the summer associate next to him.

"Man, I feel like my soul is floating in and out of me—I try to stick it there," he pinned the air, "like a pinned insect. Sometimes I care about others. Their fates and feelings. Sometimes I feel like shit for using women," Raul said.

"Dude—what are you talking about?" the summer asked. "Holy shit! What happened your arm! Jesus!"

"Bug bite. Nothing serious. I was just um scratching it and it bled a little. Um, do you think. Did you see Judith throw her shot glass over into the street?"

"Man, Judith is a dirty sock," the summer said.

"A what?" Raul asked.

"You know. You were a junior high school boy—your dirty sock. That's Judith. Go for it, if you like."

"No, I just didn't hear the first time. Man, that's gross. That's hysterical. Ms. Merewether, did you hear what he just said? Ms. Merewether?"

She was turned away from him, talking to a firm partner.

She turned. "Yes Raul?"

Raul saw Ms. Merewether had been strumming his back like a guitar. Even seeing her touching him, he could not feel her fingers until he concentrated. When he finally felt her touch, his skin tingled pleasantly.

"Uhhh. Did you know that giant bullfrogs eat their own children for food? But the tadpoles stay close anyway, for protection from other predators."

"No, Raul. I didn't know that."

"I saw it—I learned it at a frog exhibit. At the history museum. Strange—playing the odds like that. Isn't it? What awards did we win today?"

"Women's Rights Leadership and Environmentally Friendly Law Firm of the Year."

"Impressive."

"Yes. It is."

"Oh shit. Oh shit. Wait. Wait. I have to call my parents and tell them I'm not coming home tonight."

"Oh. Yes you do, yes you do," Ms. Merewether said. She patted his chest then reached into his jacket, pulled out his phone and put it into his hand. "Guys. Guys. Everyone has to be quiet. Raul has to call his parents to tell them he's not making it home tonight." The crowd quieted and looked at Raul. The room became so quiet they could hear the other line ringing.

"Hello," a gruff voice said on the other end.

"Hi Dad. I'm not coming home tonight. I'm aaah staying with some friends. I don't think can phtha—you know. I think it's better if I just stay with some friends."

"Uh, Raul, you know you're in New York City, right?"

"Right," Raul said. "Yes sir."

"Son, you also know, we—your mother and I—live in California now."

"Right. Right. Yes sir." He snapped his cellphone shut and looked up at everyone. "That was not fucking funny guys."

The room broke into laughter.

"Guys, you don't understand, my father is a fucking important general in the fucking U.S. military. And he's going to be pissed tomorrow. He's going to fucking find me and all of you, and blow our houses up." Raul made an exploding sound, then looked down at his bloody bandages. The purpled skin around the sacks was sweaty. He could feel the spider eggs start to pulse in rhythm with his heartbeat. "Okay. It's kind of funny. Okay. It's funny."

About the Author

Timothy DeLizza was raised in Brooklyn, NY and currently resides in Washington, DC. He has previously been published in several literary magazines, including most recently in the *Zodiac Review* and *Pif Magazine*. You can find him at http://www.timothy-delizza.com.

Surfing between 500 Foreign Channels

By Elena V. Molina

Translated by George Bert Henson

Interviews

A group of people respond to the same interview question: "What is democracy?" Later the recording of their voices and faces is cut into small pieces and ordered in such a way that they give a continuous speech written by the editor. Nevertheless, the fragmentation of the image is inevitable and the effect of their faces, visible for a second on the surface of the celluloid, able to say only a word-contraction-article, is reminiscent of someone drowning gasping for air.

Scriptwriters

Two people being interviewed are opponents who make up part of the same game system. They disagree in matters of oppressor and oppressed. The One has the truth, against the Other and the world. The ironic Other calmly does his own thing and smiles. The One, frustrated and cranky, makes threats the whole time and talks about himself a lot. The Other smiles. They're litigating authorship. The reporter seems sure which one is right.

Sortie de secours | Emergency Exit

A woman appears running in a basement | runs into the person who was waiting for her | they argue | and she chooses one of the exits. The pursuer appears. He utters the name and points to the door. He utters the name (averting his eyes). Utters the name (shouts). Utters the name (doesn't move his lips). Utters the name and trembles. Utters the name (grabbing his head) and then shoots himself with a gun. Utters the name as he falls. The woman who is waiting stares straight ahead.

He Who Doesn't Speak

Someone in a café is about to speak. The image freezes. Someone in a car's about to speak. The image freezes. Someone in an auditorium's about to speak. The image freezes. Someone walking on the sidewalk's about to speak. The image freezes. Someone in a movie theater's about to speak. The image freezes. Someone in a club's about to speak. The image freezes. Someone in the shower's about to speak. The image freezes. Someone's about to speak. The image freezes.

Security Camera

People cross at the corner and look to the left. Cars pass on the right without stopping for the girls thumbing a ride. The camera focuses on them, on their license plate number. A man with a sunflower is standing in the middle of the frame. He interrupts traffic. They come and take him away.

Another day: the same people cross at the corner looking to the left. Cars pass on the right. The girls and the camera focus on the book being held by the man who's walking in the middle of traffic, interrupting it. They come and take him away.

The next day a man walks from left to right shouting at cars and passersby. They interrupt traffic, they are going to kill him.

Manolito's Show

At a café, one radio station follows another. Manolito switches from one to the next, receiving different signals at each table. People buy coffee and listen to him. They ask about the antenna he's using, ask him to play an FM station. At one table there's only interference. He remembers the sound of the electroshocks.

The Hole

The Hall-Runner wants to get out of the Hole. There's one door after another. He's a loner who's chasing the picture in the books. He never leaves the place. From time to time he visits the Dreamer and his plants. There he stares at the books all day and night, and goes out again. The stairs lead to hallways. There's one hallway after another. He has never seen the Architect's plans but at the end he finds an exit. It leads to the ocean. The Hall-Runner dives into the water.

Country House

Against a backdrop of white walls, a nude teenage girl walks by a man who's doing zazen. She goes out to the patio, squats over a drain and urinates. Raddled, the man flees. Every day she appears in a different room interrupting his routine. Someone knocks on the door. The man doesn't answer it. She crosses the threshold eating oranges.

Haciendo zapping entre 500 canales extranjeros

Entrevistas

Un grupo de personas son entrevistadas respondiendo la misma pregunta: ¿qué es Democracia? Luego sus voces y rostros grabados son picados en pequeños pedazos y ordenados de manera que dicen consecuentemente un discurso escrito por el editor. Sin embargo, la fragmentación de la imagen es inevitable y el efecto de los rostros visibles un segundo en la superficie del celuloide, pudiendo decir solo una palabra-contracción-artículo, recuerda al de los ahogados luchando por sobrevivir.

Guionistas

Dos personas entrevistadas son contrarios que forman parte del mismo sistema de juego. Se oponen en criterios de opresor y oprimido. El Uno con la verdad, contra el Otro y el mundo. El Otro irónico, tranquilo va a lo suyo y sonríe. El Uno exasperado y quejoso amenaza todo el rato y habla mucho de sí mismo. El Otro sonríe. Están en litigios de autoría. El periodista parece seguro de quién es el bueno.

Sortie de secourt | Salida de seguridad

Una mujer aparece corriendo en un sótano | choca con quien le estaba esperando | discuten | y escoge una de las puertas de salida. Aparece el perseguidor. Pronuncia el nombre y señala a la puerta. Pronuncia el nombre (quitando los ojos). Pronuncia el nombre (grita). Pronuncia el nombre (no mueve los labios). Pronuncia el nombre y tiembla. Pronuncia el nombre (agarrándose la cabeza) y con un arma después se dispara. Pronuncia el nombre mientras cae. La mujer que espera mantiene la mirada fija.

El que no habla

Alguien en un café va a hablar. Se congela la imagen. Alguien en un auto va hablar. Se congela la imagen. Alguien en un auditorio va hablar. Se congela la imagen. Alguien caminando en la acera va hablar. Se congela la imagen. Alguien en el cine va hablar. Se congela la imagen. Alguien en una peña va hablar. Se congela la imagen. Alguien en la ducha va hablar. Se congela la imagen. Alguien va hablar. Se congela la imagen.

Cámara de seguridad

Las personas cruzan la esquina mirando a la izquierda. Por la derecha pasan los carros sin parar a las chicas que piden botella. La cámara se fija en ellos, en su número de chapa. Un hombre con un girasol está parado en medio del cuadro, interrumpe el tráfico. Vienen y le sacan.

Otro día, las mismas personas cruzan la esquina mirando a la izquierda. Por la derecha pasan los carros. Las chicas y la cámara se fijan en un libro del hombre que se pasea por el medio e interrumpe el tráfico. Vienen y le sacan.

Al siguiente día un hombre camina de izquierda a derecha gritando a la gente que pasa y a los carros. Interrumpen el tráfico. Van a matarle.

Manolito's Show

En el café las emisoras de radio se suceden. Manolito cambia de una a otra recibiendo de las mesas diferentes señales. La gente compra café y lo escucha. Hacen preguntas sobre qué antena emplea. Le piden FM. En una mesa hay solo interferencia. Recuerda el sonido de los electrochocks.

El Hueco

El Corre Pasillos quiere salir del hueco. Las puertas se suceden. Es un solitario que persigue la imagen de los libros. No sale del lugar. De vez en vez visita al Soñador y a sus plantas. Allí mira los libros todo el día y la noche, vuelve a salir. Las escaleras desembocan en pasillos. Los pasillos se suceden. Nunca ha visto las plantas del Arquitecto pero finalmente encuentra una salida. Da al mar. El Corre Pasillos salta al agua.

Casa de campo

Una adolescente se pasea desnuda frente al hombre haciendo zazen. De fondo las paredes blancas. La chica va al patio, se agacha sobre un tragante y orina. Él huye desencajado. Todos los días en cada habitación ella aparece interrumpiendo su rutina. Alguien llama a la puerta. El hombre no atiende. Ella cruza el umbral comiendo naranjas.

About the Author

Cuban writer and filmmaker Elena V. Molina (Cuba 1988) currently resides in Barcelona where she is the managing editor for Linkgua publishing. In her spare time, she is the Creative Director of the Muestra de Cine Independiente Cubano de Barcelona. In Cuba she was, together with Raul Flores, the cofounder and publisher of the literary magazine *33 y 1/3* from 2005-2011. Since 2007 she has collaborated in the organization and programming of Cuban film festivals and exhibits in Cuba, Argentina, Germany, and Spain. She studied Audiovisual Communication in Havana and Buenos Aires.

About the Translator

George Bert Henson is a translator of contemporary Spanish prose. His translations include works by some of Latin America's and Spain's most notable writers, including Sergio Pitol, Elena Poniatowska, Andrés Neuman, Claudia Salazar, Miguel Barnet, and Leonardo Padura, and have appeared variously in *Words Without Borders*, *Buenos Aires Review*, *Bomb*, *Asymptote*, *The Kenyon Review*, and *World Literature Today*, where he is a contributing editor. His translations of Sergio Pitol's *The Art of Flight* and *The Journey* were published last year by Deep Vellum Publishing. George teaches in the Department of Spanish & Portuguese at the University of Illinois Urbana-Champaign, where he is also affiliated with the Center for Translation Studies. He holds a PhD from the University of Texas at Dallas.

catalogue cards
(from cape breton university)

By Sean Howard

i. the conquest of the river plate

pampas, horses
ford the stream… (

waves making the land
fall.) silence: conduct-

ing the dead. night
& day; silver &

gold

ii. gandhi and king

sleep: 'hate in their
eyes.' (white god, black

maria.) hindu or muslim? the
rain's temples… trampled; bat-

on rouge. shared feast;
eyes on the hori-

zon

iii. can prisons work?

inner cities. (on res.; indian territory.) poem: white-

wash. 'in the end, your own
cell.' violence: keeping the

inside out. forest–
throw away the

key

iv. the human species

science; pry
mates. (King Con-

quest.) graduation; 'apelike
beings.' full circle: tidepool,

man reflecting… genes
slowly making

love?

About the Author

Sean Howard is the author of *Local Calls* (Cape Breton University Press, 2009) and *Incitements* (Gaspereau Press, 2011). His poetry has been widely published in Canada, the US, UK and elsewhere, and anthologized in *The Best Canadian Poetry in English* (Tightrope Books, 2011 & 2014).

Imagining Havana

By Alicita Rodríguez

Havana is a city of doors and windows, an array of rectangles and rhombuses. Transom windows inside crumbling mansions let breezes blow from room to room. Ocean winds push from sea to salon, cooling Nando, who sleeps in his hammock. He is framed by the patio doors, sectioned by the kitchen window, furcated by the bathroom jalousies. Those who can fly see his cubist face disappear as they rise—until he becomes a pin in the street grid, a mere dot at the junction of Neptuno and Espada. Nando too can fly. He uses the transom windows as a passage, slipping into and through and out of the open lozenges. They are like the arcades of Paris or the catacombs of Rome. The flying inhabitants drift and coast through French doors and Moroccan arches. But others stay put in their hot houses, knowing they can only fly within the city limits. That is the fenestration of Havana.

Imagining Sancti Spíritus

The dancing bears of Sancti Spíritus show up at inopportune times. During mass at Parroquial Mayor, for instance, where their kicks cause the thurible to swing wildly on its chain. Amid this pendulum of plumes, we suffer the clouds of frankincense. So aromatic we feel as if we have eaten Mama's soap. When we are in a hurry at the *mercado*, squeezing the mangoes and searching for ripe plantains, they captivate the shopkeeper with their tinkling anklets and ruffled skirts, making us late for dinner. On lazy afternoons while we nap in hammocks on the banks of the Yayabo, the ursine prancers wake us from dreams of revenge. They shuffle into the movie theater during matinees of *The Crimson Kimono*, contaminating our popcorn with the smell of musk. In the mornings, we sometimes find their fur on our pillows.

Imagining Cienfuegos

Perhaps because of the French influence, Cienfuegos is a city dominated by outlandish color. It is called the Pearl of the South for its beauty. It should have been called the Mother of Pearl of the South, for its painted houses. There is a neoclassical *farmacia* festooned with bas-relief scrolls that is a cloying shade of mint. A cyan hotel, a cathedral in goldenrod, a violet girl's school, and a great green mansion. Every year they paint the Arco de Triunfo a different brown. It has been wheat and lion; sand, copper, and fawn. Next year they have proposed liver. Some *universitarios* started a campaign to paint the triumphant arch Baker-Miller Pink, a color invented by two Navy officers who tested its effect on sailors. When they painted prison cells in the pink, they recorded "no incidents of erratic or hostile behavior." Even if the coloring campaign succeeded, and the arch were dripping in Baker-Miller, it would remain unpalatable. The subduing effect lasts only "during the initial phase of confinement." And the confinement of the residents of Cienfuegos is well beyond that.

About the Author

Alicita Rodríguez is a Cuban-American writer born and raised in Miami. Her fiction, poetry, and nonfiction have been published in *Sentence*, *TriQuarterly*, *Palabra*, and *Sudden Fiction Latino*, among others.

Fox, Húlí

By Kelly Werrell

狐狸

"The landscape is a moment of time // that has gotten into position."
—Lyn Hejinian, "The Guard."

In each moment, she was digging a smaller and smaller hole until she came upon a skeleton, and time for a moment stopped. The skeleton was a curved, small body, and it lay there at the bottom. The holes Julie had been digging lay around them like craters. The holes were shallow and the dirt was not compact, so digging was easy. The skeleton lay at the bottom and appeared mostly intact. She used the fingertip of her glove to dust off the skull. The skull was small and round, about the size of her palm. She held her palm over the skull comparing them. There was energy in her palm. It came up from the skull in waves then retracted back inside. She removed her glove. The skull sent out activity, electricity, magnetism, and it shot through her hand up into her body, into her own skull, and that was when the ghost arrived inside her.

The ghost filled her up like a handful of marbles rolling around through her appendages then settling. When it settled in her head she felt the tiny glass balls clink behind her ears and eyes, resting in the lacunae. The glass was cool. It gave her a headache.

The sun dipped behind the mountain and the work bell sounded. Julie looked into the hole and the skeleton lay there inert.

1. She lifted the skeleton into her apron and draped her jacket over it. It fell apart instantly and the bones clacked together in the big pocket as she walked. She walked deliberately around the holes.

2. She covered it loosely with dirt. The hole appeared complete, so she left it.

3. The wind blew, blowing dust into her mouth. The dirt spun in the hole like a tornado and lifted the skeleton up. It stood on its own in the tornado until the tornado died. Then it sat down and aimed its eye sockets at Julie. She imagined threading a black ribbon through the sockets.

Húlí, said the ghost. It spoke from behind her eyes. She felt its mouth cup around her brain. The valley was wide and yellow. It spread out until the mountains then turned brown and rose sharply upward. The holes faded across the expanse. Dust blew and the sky was gray. The dust blew up into the sky and the sky blew back down onto the earth, spreading the soot and particles like a film over the ground. The mountains were dark and heavy. The mountains loomed high, went outward for miles, and blocked the rise and set of the sun.

1. The ghost used its powers to reassemble the skeleton in her pocket. She could feel it shifting and hear it clicking into place. The ghost showed the inside of her pocket in her mind's eye. Bones wiggled together. It formed into the shape of an animal. The bones were very, very small. The ghost was pulsing in her, warm. It felt like the ghost was reaching out.

2. She looked back to the hole and the dirt appeared dark, loose, and convex above it.

3. The skeleton looked at her. The landscape was frozen in time. There was no wind, no sun. Her coworkers, spread out along the valley floor, were motionless in work. Shovels were in the ground or hovering above it, bodies bent over or standing. The dust in the air hung. She imagined picking up the little skull and holding it in her hand, wearing it as a talisman. The skeleton looked at her. Julie stood still, unsure of whether or not she was mobile. At once her body rose, her feet off the ground, and then she was set down again. The skeleton copied the motion. It raised its little arm and Julie raised hers. It tilted its head and so did she. Time was passing in small, infinite increments. Nothing was happening. Julie looked at the skeleton and the skeleton looked back.

Everywhere was dust. A fox walked along the valley floor looking for prey. It dug at holes and sniffed small, hearty plants.

About the Author

Kelly Werrell has an MFA from the University of San Francisco. She lives in Colorado. "Fox, Huli" was partially conceived while traveling in China and reading *Strange Tales from a Chinese Studio* by Pu Songling.

Broken Chord

By Lillian-Yvonne Bertram & Steve Davenport

You are the woman

from the television show who would rather

be sedated than cry—my one friend

always this species of correct

analysis and application, all eye

and murder where blues concern.

Yesterday went wrong and tomorrow's

a scene you won't want to live to. Like the queer

girls who bite the bitter stream of marriage

and manage, we sharpen our thirteen ways,

blackbirds scattering back into focus, before

we leap into what little moonlight

can romance—*He said he God*—

and fall, butcher scraps for tubs,

offal for new skewers.

About the Authors

Lillian-Yvonne Bertram is the author of *But a Storm is Blowing From Paradise* (Red Hen Press), chosen by Claudia Rankine as winner of the 2010 Red Hen Press Benjamin Saltman Award, *a slice from the cake made of air* (Red Hen Press), and the forthcoming *personal science* (Tupelo). She teaches at the University of Massachusetts—Boston.

A product of American Bottom, an Illinois floodplain across the Mississippi from St. Louis, Steve Davenport is the author of two poetry collections: *Overpass* (2012) and *Uncontainable Noise* (2006). His poems, stories, and essays have been anthologized, reprinted, and published in scores of literary magazines both on-line and in print. A recent story in *The Southern Review* received a 2011 Pushcart Prize Special Mention. *His Murder on Gasoline Lake*, published in *Black Warrior Review* and later as a chapbook, is listed as Notable in Best American Essays 2007. At AWP Chicago in 2009, he had the honor of organizing and moderating a tribute to William Gass with participants Mary Jo Bang, Kathryn Davis, Gordon Hutner, and Rikki Ducornet. His scholarship includes essays about the Beat Generation, Jack Kerouac, and Richard Hugo. Recently he's gotten involved in songwriting projects. One example is *Art Box Collective*. Another is the collaborative work he's done with Bruce "Bruiser" Rummenie on *This Noise in My Blood*, a CD of seven songs.

Davenport has also co-authored with wife Lynn four daughters, ages 15, 13, 11, and 7 (their names, One, Two, That's It, and This Isn't Funny Anymore). He likes his coffee black and his George Dickel (Old No. 8) poured hard over chipped ice in his favorite glass. His mantra? If he had one? Whiskey cleans the whiskey glass. You can find him on Facebook and at his shiny new website Gasoline Lake.

Madam Angel

By Ihsan Abdel Quddous

Translated by Nabeel Yaseen

I will never forget Madam Angel. Months might pass without my having any thought of her—but suddenly, while I sit at the dinner table or perhaps walk out of my office, I see her rawboned face in my mind. She had a dry, feeble body, like a thin metal skewer. In my fantasies I remember her vivid eyes, her hard, sweaty hands, and the light hair barely visible above her lips and scattered on her chin, even covering her arms. The constant frown on her lips reflected her permanent state of resentment. She spoke Arabic with a Greek accent.

When I was a child, Madam Angel would come to our house and spend the entire day knitting clothes for my mother. My mother delighted in her coming and prepared different types of food, especially the long macaroni she called "spaghetti" that she served with roasted meat and fino bread. Whenever I saw macaroni in the kitchen, I knew that Madam Angel would dine with us. Although Madam Angel was indeed one of the most skillful seamstresses in the neighborhood, I think my mother's interest in her mainly arose from her belief that Madam Angel was a Westerner or foreigner. And so my mother prepared foreign foods for her and adopted foreign behaviors, trying to act like Madam Angel. I watched my mother deliberately using foreign words when she talked to her—silly words that had nothing to do with the conversation such as *bonjour*, *merci*, *corset*, and *papillon*.

When Madam Angel spoke, my mother listened breathlessly, as if she were hearing Platonic wisdom, as if she were standing before a new city whose closed gates would open into a new life for her. Madam Angel was quite aware of her influence on my mother, and took advantage of it by cultivating a sort of intimate friendship with her. Madam Angel would visit us regularly, spending the whole day with us but with no intention of knitting clothes. She controlled us, and my kind-hearted mother surrendered to her, fascinated by her foreign accent. My quiet father often smiled sarcastically, leaving Madam Angel to treat my mother however she wanted.

Madam Angel was pompous, making it clear that she abhorred how we lived. She constantly gave commands and advice, supposedly trying to elevate us to the *beau monde* in which she claimed to live.

Once she entered my room while I was sleeping and found the window closed; she yelled in her Greek accent, ordering my mother, "Madam, this is wrong! This window should remain open to let the fresh air come in for the boy. When my daughter Maria sleeps, she always leaves her window open!" My mother loved Ms. Angel's addressing her as "Madam." The title made her feel "khawaja"—high class—like Madam Angel herself. My mother immediately opened the window, and, although I shivered from the cold, I dared not object.

Once, Madam Angel saw me eating mulukhiyah by dipping bread into the bowl and then placing it in my mouth. She shouted, "Not this way, darling! We also cook mulukhiyah in our house, but we eat it with spoons like soup. My daughter Maria eats it with a spoon, so you should be like Maria!" My mother and I therefore ate mulukhiyah with a spoon.

On another occasion, Madam Angel looked at me with keen eyes and said,

"You don't look very healthy; you should drink some cinchona juice. My daughter Maria drinks one cup of cinchona juice every day, and her cheeks are as red as blood." My mother then forced me to drink it despite my objection and my crying.

Neither my mother nor I ever saw Maria, Madam Angel's daughter. She never visited our house despite my mother's many requests; nor did we visit hers. Perhaps my mother thought that meeting Maria was an honor we didn't deserve. I spent hours fantasizing what Maria was like. I imagined her with long blonde hair, with red cheeks and a white, rounded, healthy face. Whenever I saw a picture of a little girl in a magazine, I thought Maria must be like that. I imagined her to be such a very, very strong girl that I became frightened of her. I imagined her not getting pertussis, measles, flu, or any other disease I had experienced. I always thought of her as a very clean girl who didn't play our games, or eat the way we did, or talk the way we talked. I imagined her as an angel who didn't live on earth.

Maria became the center of my life, because Madam Angel always advised me to do whatever Maria did. My mother would beat me and tell me that Maria was younger than me, yet she still did everything better than me. Embittered, I hated and feared her, yet I still wished to see her.

Then came a seemingly long series of days during which Madam Angel never visited our house. After two weeks, she showed up again— dressed in black, her formerly hard body withered, her previously strong voice weak and fallen.

"What happened, Madam Angel?" my mother asked.

Crying, she replied, "My daughter Maria!"

"What's wrong with her?" my mother asked, slapping her chest.

While tears poured out of her eyes, Madam Angel said, "Finished … morto!"

My mother began to cry. "Died … how did she die?"

Madam Angel said, "She had anemia!"

My mother looked at me and hugged me, as if she was protecting me from death. I looked at Madam Angel, not believing what she said. She kept crying and talking to us about Maria. Then, she took Maria's photo from her bag and handed it to us. My mother and I anxiously looked at the photo. We were surprised to see a weak, thin, and yellow face.

My life changed completely after Maria's death. My mother closed the windows when I slept, and would tell me to eat mulukhiyah with bread to gain weight. She stopped giving me cinchona juice. My mother was finally liberated from Madam Angel's domination, and forgot about her.

But I still remembered.

About the Author

Ihsan Abdel Quddous is an Egyptian writer, novelist, and journalist. He is known to have written many novels that have been adapted in films.

About the Translator

Dr. Nabeel M Yaseen holds a PhD in English Literature and Criticism from Indiana University of Pennsylvania, a Master of English literature and composition from the University of Akron-Ohio. He taught at various universities in the US and the Middle East. Dr. Yaseen taught at the University of Illinois at Urbana-Champaign and Pennsylvania State University. Now, he is an assistant professor at Qassim University where he teaches English literature and translation. He is interested in the 19th and 20th century American literature and literary translation; especially, the literary works of Ihsan Abdel Quddous and other Arab writers.

Where the Buffalo Roam

By Keith Stahl

Marne didn't believe that Geoff saw a buffalo in the woods behind the cemetery. He could tell because he got the same distracted *I believe* she always gave on Sunday mornings when he switched her over from the TV evangelists to *NFL Today*.

You can't really believe this stuff.

I believe.

She didn't really.

He was going to come home and wrap Marne in a buffalo blanket. *Believe me now?* He could taste it. He'd sell the head to Mr. Duke, and Mr. Duke would hang it in the diner. Geoff would run specials: Bison Burger. Buffalo Stew. The *Dispatch* would interview Geoff, take pictures, full-color spread about bison making a comeback in Central New York. They'd beg for Geoff's Buffaloaf recipe.

He'd sell it to them.

Geoff swatted at the bugs. Pointless. They hovered just beyond reach, biding their time, toying. He picked at a droning deer fly plugging his ear. They were brilliant, the way they got into his head. The woods were sick with them.

Geoff probed the muck, fingered his Croc, drew it out with a squishy *slurp*.

Marne had gotten so complicated. Like the mud that kept sucking off Geoff's shoes.

Geoff and Marne once kissed on Kiss Cam. Why couldn't it still be like that? Their boss at Applebee's gave Geoff tickets for Inclusion Night at the Chief's game. *It won't be a date*, Geoff assured Marne. But everyone hooted, *Broomhilda and The Mange!* She didn't say yes or no. She never said anything. She hardly left the dish cave. She snorted, sometimes, when Geoff dangled carrots from his nose, *I am the walrus, goo goo g'joob*. But after the shift, Marne was milling around Geoff's truck like used furniture left on the curb, so he just put her in the cab. In the seventh inning, Geoff cocked his head to watch his own Jumbotronned face kissing Marne's clenched lips. He lingered for the camera. Bugs were swarming the lights because they thought it was the sun, or something.

The crowd went *Ooooooo.* Marne snorted. A freight train clacked by the left-field fence, and Geoff told Marne the diesel horn sounded like it was saying *Hello.* Marne said, "Hello." Geoff put his arm around her chair, kept it there through the ninth inning. Even after it fell asleep.

The gloppy fire road was starting to smell like muggy sewage. People got hard-ons for nature. Why?

It was like Geoff didn't know Marne anymore. He remembered looking forward to Marne's face: He was jerking open this storage locker he had purchased at auction. It was dangling with dream catchers.

She was gushing, *Are you sure this is all right?*

Finders, keepers.

Marne said it must have been a mistake. Someone forgot these porcelain dolls, heirlooms peeking from a shroud of *Time* magazines. "Some little girl loved these."

She was oblivious to the dream catchers.

Marne nestled the dolls throughout the house; they lolled about in chairs, on the sofa, in the bed. Geoff crushed one, sitting in the recliner. Marne's face was plastic, like she was all right, but she wasn't all right. Somehow that made Geoff go *click.*

Geoff had this switch. Sometimes Marne threw it. Sometimes it *click*ed for no reason. Sometimes it was Buffalo. The Bills would lose, and Geoff would turn off the TV, *click,* and lose himself in the black. The Bills lost a lot.

He'd rant about having to live in a dilapidated trailer on an Indian reservation with his squaw.

It's a mobile home.

Marne grew up in this house.

You grew up in a dump.

She'd hide in the bathroom.

Geoff had installed the light switch in the bathroom. It sparked if you weren't gentle. He'd hover outside the bathroom door to hear her yelp.

You. Have. To. Be. Gentle.

I'm all right.

You're not all right.

Geoff would come into the dark bathroom to fix her.

It's not you, he'd say. *It's the beer. It's the Bills. Buffalo sucks so bad.*

And Marne would stroke Geoff's bristled hair, finger-tipping patches of bald. She'd tell him about the bus home from school, when she was nine, and how boys secretly tied her scraggly hair into knots. How she cried on the toilet while her mother sheared away the tangles.

Then Marne would make chicken tetrazzini.

Geoff's feet slurped and splashed in the bubbling casserole, but he stayed with the muddy fire road. It was too hot and sticky to get lost.

Marne was unpredictable. She started panicking. The first panic was at her mother's funeral. *Who the hell leaves a suicide tweet?* Marne panicked at the mall, Walmart, the post office. She flapped like a chicken at Dairy Queen, *I can't breathe,* while Geoff clasped her wrists, *You can breathe.* Everybody was yowling, *Oh my God! She can't breathe!* But Geoff assured them all, *She can breathe.* After that, Geoff never went to Dairy Queen, and Marne never went anywhere. Not work, even. But it wasn't like she appreciated it. Mondays still felt like Mondays, Marne said. Every day felt like Monday.

Geoff had scored a storage locker full of Lunesta, Ambien, Valium, and Xanax. He sold some at Duke's Diner, where he had started working after Applebee's accused him of stealing American cheese; but mostly he doled the pills out to Marne in portion-cups. He warned her to save them for when she really needed, like bedtimes, but Marne ferreted out one of Geoff's stashes in the garage. He came home to empty containers scattered among fourteen cases of votive candles. Marne locked herself in the bathroom. She never locked herself in the bathroom. She kept whimpering, *I'm all right.*

You're not all right.

Geoff spent all night getting Marne out of there. She couldn't figure the lock. It was scary.

Cicadas wouldn't shut up. Geoff didn't know what they were, but wanted to shoot the motherfuckers.

Geoff owned trophies, two deer heads and a rhinoceros, from a storage locker he bought. He learned the rhino was *faux,* but he planned to sell it as *real.* (This shotgun was real. He could tell by the ammo.) His garage was starting to smell like mating season, from the deer heads. He wasn't moving product. He figured Swap Sheet customers were calling, but couldn't get through because Marne was on the phone all day shopping QVC. Geoff was channel surfing one night while Marne was asleep, and the woman who's all teeth on Home Shopping Network actually said, *Marne, if you're out there, you're going to love Jesus In A Box!* So Geoff got Marne to watch *Hoarders* with him, kind of like an intervention, but she kept flipping during the commercials. Three days later, UPS came with twenty-seven college mascot nutcrackers.

Geoff jumped at a squirrel.

There was this Schwan's guy. When Geoff and Marne ate dinner, Marne wrote down how much chicken tetrazzini they were eating, how much chicken was left in the freezer, how many peas. Marne applied makeup only on Schwan's delivery day, and she watched QVC with no sound so she could hear the Schwan's truck.

Geoff heard them giggling at the door. Worse. They were trying not to giggle. There was something hysterically funny about frozen peas.

"The peas are working out okay, then?"

"Yes. My husband enjoys the tiny onions."

Geoff caught a glimpse. The Schwan's guy had his thumbs hooked in his belt. He wasn't even taking Marne's order. It was bullshit.

After that, Geoff didn't feel so bad about Cassandra. Maybe Cassandra was meant to be.

Geoff had been pulling pork one morning when Cassandra first pedaled by the diner window. The Unicorn Unicyclist. Sequined and shiny, wigwagging along the sidewalk, flourishing purple pinwheels, milky white hair big and bushy, bloated leotard. She rigged the unicycle with a stick horse that had a horn. Her ass swallowed the bike seat.

Geoff stabbed himself, throbbed and bled into the shredded meat.

He timed it so he was setting the outside tables every morning, ready for Cassandra with things to say. *Where's your yellow jersey?* Her smile was like Borax. *You're missing a wheel.* She bobbed like the Famous Drinking Bird. *Great day for THAT!*

It became a thing.

We have to stop meeting like this, he said one morning. And she stopped. She stopped!

Are you the owner?

Sure.

I know you're not open, but I am parched.

And he let her in. He gave her bottled water, because the diner water wasn't really triple-filtered. He told her how the smoked pulled pork wasn't really smoked. He showed her a gallon of Liquid Smoke that was hidden behind the register. He told her how he installed his own security system at home, but the real deterrent were the ADT Security stickers in the windows. He knew a guy at ADT Security. He told her how kids used to call him The Mange. He told her how he knew a guy at Nobody's Business Storage Units who let him inside storage units, sometimes, before an auction.

You watch Storage Wars?

Not really.

It's nothing like that.

He told her there were twenty-three hundred dollars in a Pop Tart box in his kitchen at home; the VISA was good for another twelve hundred; his checking account was overdrawn, but Mr. Duke hadn't gone to the bank yesterday so there had to be three, four hundred bucks sitting in the register. He'd been thinking about just *going.*

Who's Mr. Duke?

This guy who works for me.

Cassandra smirked at Geoff's wedding ring. *Is your wife coming, too?*

It was like getting caught making Lobster Bisque with imitation crab.

Geoff shelled out a hundred and eighty bucks to join the Y. He told Marne the Y was about losing weight.

Why do you want to lose weight?

He offered to get her a membership, too. He knew she'd say no. She hadn't left the house in two and a half years.

Geoff tried to surprise Cassandra at her cycling class, her *spinning* class, but it wasn't even her. It was a substitute. A dark room full of twigs with expensive haircuts who didn't sweat. *Woot! Woot!* Lady Gaga. He just stewed in the hot tub.

The rush of Bullshit Falls made Geoff stop. It only had water after it rained. It had been dry last week, when Geoff was searching for arrowheads (or anything he could sell as arrowheads), so he had been able to hear it then: the crackle of a deer, a squirrel, a stray dog.

It was a monster. The Devil on all fours.

He ran.

He hadn't run since eighth grade gym class. It was like breathing ammonia. He was off the fire road, prickers and whippersnappers lashing his face. He staggered from the bushes, by sheer luck onto the manicured lawn of the cemetery, blinded by stinging sweat, bungling his keys. He unlocked the door on the third try. The truck stammered and spit, thundered, finally lurched away in an eye-stinging cloud of exhaust.

He didn't look back.

That giant head.

The answer came, back in Geoff's garage, in a stack of Mylar-wrapped *Nature Friend* magazines.

It was a buffalo, bison, whatever.

He had heard at the diner that black bears were roaming south from the Adirondacks. Cougars, Bald Eagles, and now buffalo. "Buffalo" was "Buffalo" because of all the buffalo.

The Indians.

It all came together.

They didn't believe him. Mr. Duke said buffalo were distinct; you had to go out west. And Marne said she believed, yeah yeah yeah. He wasn't sure about Cassandra. He wasn't even sure himself anymore.

He'd never hear a buffalo over the cascade. Approaching the falls, he crouched, slowed to a crawl.

He literally stumbled upon Cassandra.

It was karma.

"Cassandra?

She sat like a garden statue. Geisha, Buddha, whatever. A flat boulder was set with rotting apples. Geoff had saved them for her, from the diner. He assumed she had a horse, rabbits, maybe an alpaca.

"Geoff?"

Cassandra pouted at Geoff's shotgun. She whined like porn. "Are you going to shoot me?"

"Having a picnic?"

"I didn't know you were a hunter."

"Want to see my trophies?"

Cassandra rearranged the apples on the rock, and Geoff could see her wrinkled balloons. It was kind of hot that they weren't real.

She caught him looking. She turned away and smiled.

"Join me?"

The apples were starting to look like turds, but Geoff would eat turds if Cassandra told him to eat turds.

"I'm not flexible," he said. "I don't think I can sit like you." He laughed, bleated, like a sheep, supported himself with the butt of the shotgun to unload his three hundred pounds onto the ground. He hadn't loaded the shotgun because he wasn't sure how the safety worked.

"It's wet," he said.

"Be still." Cassandra raised her hand. She had rings on all her fingers. Thumb rings.

The bugs weren't bothering her. They swarmed Geoff like a halo.

Geoff watched Cassandra watching the apples. It was like Cassandra's lips were inflated.

Her eyes widened, like one of Marne's panics. Her lips went, *Oh!*

There was a chipmunk on the rock. It held an apple. It nibbled. Slowly, at first. Teasingly. Then an oral deluge deeper and deeper into the apple.

Geoff shifted his sweatpants, and the chipmunk was gone.

"Why would you want to shoot a beautiful creature like that?" she said.

"Sometimes, it's you or the chipmunk. You'll thank me when a buffalo decides it's apples for lunch."

"You're so cute," she said.

So he went on. About bears.

"You're a big bear."

About cougars and bald eagles.

"You make me laugh."

About how he sometimes pretended he'd just murdered his wife and was running from the police.

"Oh, my." Cassandra giggled. "Can you get your hands on a dance pole?"

"Dance pole?"

"You know. That dancers use?"

"Dancers?"

"Strippers."

"I ..."

"I want one installed in my studio. Pole dancing is amazing exercise. Flexibility, cardio, resistance, emotional healing."

Geoff told her he'd install a pole within the week.

"That fast?"

"I want lessons."

"We can teach your wife to pole dance."

"That's not happening," Geoff said, machine-gun laugh. He told Cassandra how Marne just lay there.

Cassandra asked if they'd tried feathers, *Fifty Shades of Grey,* essential oils. She sold essential oils. She'd bring samples to the diner.

Geoff imagined Cassandra's vegan body pinned against the diner wall, freshly mounted buffalo head, hair wild with the smell of pulled pork.

Then it appeared. Like a dog without a chain. That split second of eye contact.

Good dog. Good dog.

A molting mountain through the trees.

"My God," said Cassandra.

It grunted, growled, like something getting sucked down the drain. Eyes rolling white. Horns.

The buffalo charged. It knocked apples off the rock. It sloshed through the stream after Cassandra and her jangling, tambourine jewelry. Then it looped back towards the easier target.

Geoff cantered down the fire road that ran from the cemetery, shotgun out like a peace offering.

Even in his panic, Geoff couldn't get his mind off Cassandra's jeggings. From sitting on the ground, there was a wet spot.

Geoff sank into the mire. He was stuck.

He turned.

The buffalo had stopped, like it didn't know what or who to chase anymore.

Rummaging through storage lockers felt like pulling a fast one over on dead people. Dead people were idiots for dying and leaving all this great stuff behind. But who had the last laugh? In Geoff's garage, customers would look through him like he were a ghost, *ooh* and *ahh* at the Stickley chairs, the ivory cameos, all the used but perfectly good. The dead had been hunters. Geoff merely scavenged. His buffalo trophy would hang in the diner forever, or someone would find it in some dusty storage unit or garage, someday. They'd want to know the story behind it. They'd want to know Geoff's story.

He unbolted the shotgun. He fumbled with a pocket full of ammunition, all shapes and sizes, like loose change. He dropped something into the breech. He slid the bolt forward and locked it into place. He raised the gun to fire.

Geoff wondered where Cassandra was. He wanted her to see this.

The shotgun twitched and bucked and burst, exploded, shattered into metallic and woody shards. Red splattered. Geoff dropped the gun. It was alive.

Was Geoff's face on fire?

Geoff ran, abandoning his shoe to the muck. The buffalo ran. They both ran away from the blast.

"Smells like coconut."

"It's a hybrid."

Geoff was going to break it. He was stuck in Cassandra's rodeo clown car.

Cassandra helped him. Ankle bracelets, bangles, armlets, rings. When this was over, he was going to surprise her with a vintage Circus Barbie.

Cassandra wrangled Geoff up the front stoop. She tripped on a porcelain skunk.

"Skunk is my spirit animal."

Marne spied through the storm door window. She opened the door. Marne and Cassandra. It was like a blinking contest.

Geoff bobbled his muddled head, tried to focus his good eye. The other eye was a purple slit. Blood pooled on his chin, dripped onto his "Got MILF?" T-shirt.

"He couldn't drive. He wouldn't go to the hospital."

Marne received Geoff into the house. It was like signing for a package.

Marne still didn't believe him, about the buffalo. She concentrated too hard on wiping the gash on his chin with iodine, refusing to look at the black eye. Maybe she wanted to believe, but couldn't help thinking *bar fight*.

"Cassandra seen the buffalo, too."

"And she's just somebody from the restaurant."

"You don't believe in me."

Marne put the top on the iodine, gathered up bandage wrappers and tape, went into the kitchen. She returned with a package of frozen peas with tiny onions.

"Put these on your eye."

"I would kill for some chicken tetrazzini."

He didn't get any. Marne went to bed early. Geoff microwaved the peas and ate them from the bag. Then he played *Left 4 Dead 2*. Marne couldn't sleep with the volume above ten.

Geoff put it at thirty-six.

He kept triggering the alarm that released the zombie hoards. He couldn't get past the sobbing zombie witch. Right joystick STAB STAB STAB.

Geoff didn't remember going to bed, but the alarm was pealing. It was like being skinned.

He escaped blankets, death-gripped a baseball bat, moved towards the bedroom door, waving the bat like Death's scythe.

A Witch was sobbing against the Illuminart landscape.

No.

She was a meth-crazed homey with a mouth full of gold.

No.

She was Marne.

She screamed.

Definitely Marne. Geoff was awake, now.

Marne pointed towards the living room. "The alarm!" She started flapping her hands, winding up for one of her panics.

And after the day he had.

Porcelain rooster figurines were batted from the shelf.

It would be an accident. He was dreaming *Left 4 Dead 2*. He thought Marne was an intruder. He'd tell Cassandra that it was the humane thing.

The bat launched Nite-Glo Jesus.

Marne squeezed her head. It was going to pop. "The alarm!"

Surprise would be her final expression. He'd see it in his sleep, every time he ate Chicken Tetrazzini.

"Geoff, are you sleepwalking?"

He'd make chicken tetrazzini for Cassandra. It would be their thing.

"Geoff, stop it! The alarm!"

It would be like putting down a pet.

"Geoff, you're scaring me!"

An innocent, *trusting* pet.

"Put down the bat!"

Marne was out the door, screaming to the bathroom.

Geoff stubbed his toe on the cast-iron Playful Pachyderms.

That alarm was always going off.

No bad guys.

All day. *A buffalo, bison, whatever.* Mr. Duke at the register, waving the *Dispatch*, a color spread of a beaming man named Chance Stolly, rifle draped across his prize, thumbs up, crooked forehead, missing teeth. *It escaped from a pen.* Bewildered customers. *It took three shots with a .270 Mosberg.* Goggling, cross-eyed buffalo. *Chance said, after he shot it, it was acting funny.* Bursts of laughter. Ding of the cash register. All day.

Cassandra never stopped at the restaurant, so Geoff tucked her apples under his shirt to sneak past Mr. Duke. He brought them to the Y.

Women with their hands in the air herded through the pool. They didn't look half bad, at least from the neck up, at least through the glass.

Cassandra strutted on the deck to echoing dance music in a one-piece skirty. The women rhythmically pointed to Geoff in the window. She tiptoed to the door and cracked it open.

Geoff smirked towards the pool. "Hands up, don't shoot! Am I right?"

"Keep moving, girls."

"Thought you might be needing these." He dangled the apples.

"And I got a line on dance poles."

"God, Geoff."

The women started to mass at one end of the pool.

"You're sweet, Geoff." Cassandra looked like a PETA poster. "But, I can't."

It felt like indigestion.

"Maybe bake Marne a pie, or something?"

Like something coming up.

Cassandra closed the door.

Do you believe in life after love? ... after love ... after love ...

Marne had left the garage door open, again.

Geoff kicked Marne's packages at the top of the stoop. They blocked the door. They were wet. It was raining.

Geoff *was* going to bake Marne a pie. He was going to make her Chicken Tetrazzini. He hadn't borrowed ingredients from the diner, either. He purchased everything. Everything.

And a twelve-pack of Saranac Pale Ale.

He hadn't found the peas with the tiny onions.

Peas were peas.

He put the groceries on the kitchen counter. Paper, never plastic.

The TV wasn't on.

She was probably in the bathroom.

He had to fix last night, waving the bat, the savage face. Like when Marne cut her own hair that time, cut it *sassy short*, and he missed a beat before telling her he liked it.

I was confused.

The bathroom door was locked.

And after the day he had.

Marne? You all right?

Geoff went back to the kitchen, pulled *The Dispatch* from the grocery bag, brought it to the bathroom door.

Marne, I want to show you something.

But the silence felt like crushing the porcelain doll.

The grocery bag tipped on the kitchen counter, frozen peas crashing to the floor.

Marne? You all right?

About the Author

Keith Stahl's work has appeared, or is forthcoming, in *Prick of the Spindle*, *The Madison Review*, *Ghost Town*, *Per Contra*, *Euphony*, and *Corium*. He was a 2016 Pushcart Prize nominee, and is currently a non-traditional undergraduate student pursuing a degree in English and Textual Studies on the Creative Writing Track at Syracuse University.

Char's Lesson

By Michelle Lewis

Now trees have shaken in the wind where there is
no wind and you must clutch yourself.

You must toggle on your heelbone and become it.

This is how they plot the living: to rove and arc us,
take away our bough, our eros, whatever shell we breasted. To rise
the bottom up and drop it out of me.

Heart merely ash, and the Flame I'm mother to–
it clings, it takes my knees down. I cannot put more blood to it.

Char's Sorrow

The thing about my mother is I don't think
you understand *cramhole*,   I don't think you understand *back into*.

The thing is take the scissors to bed.

Is what kind of man puts candy in a dish that isn't candy but just mints.

The kind of man she's with
while I'm home, on a farm. I am eleven
      and all this seems like *brave* but really it is *breaking*.

The thing about my mother is between the flowers of the wallpaper
I have written tiny words
and jiminy   it is a garden of the body.
Of crotch and rub and feel me up. So far apart
no one could know they even   say.

All this seems like *succor*, when it is really *suck her*.

The thing about my mother is I don't think
you understand   *alone in this acreage of dark*
      where I listen in on the party line   till they say

      someone's there, someone's breathing
      to each other.

The thing about my mother
is this is one way to girl me.   One way to fear-me-not.

Is some of our stuff in his garage.

Is this body's orchard
saying   teach me how to die
while I'm still living.

Flame's Relief

Will tonight be every night?

Outside the kick-out door
saying if the dark
then so can I,   saying let someone return.

Saying this looks like *leave him* but is really *suck him*.

The dark is the best of all the ruptures. Here after the movie where they
flew off the cliff it was nothing like drowning, which is
        the best way, the hair's soft waltz, pocketful of whore-y posies.

How could I
        know? (Don't know *Eames* don't know *aioli*.)

O body, you are fresh as a daisy,
a slow rolling moss outside the drop that's bottomed.

And there it is:
flesh is merely flesh and you can empty it. You can roll
me over. Decide what is too little or too much.
Decide the shine of the nut
or the meat it tosses.
                Score it.
See how the sweetjuice takes the load off.
See the prism giving up its hues.
Fix yourself / take your gulch and plunge your fixit in.

About the Author

You can find some of Michelle's most recent poetry in *Spoon River Poetry Review, Jet Fuel Review, The Feminist Wire, Requited* (March 2016), *The Indiana Review* (Summer 2016) and *The Bennington Review* (Fall/Winter 2016). She is also the author of a forthcoming chapbook, *Who Will Be Frenchy?* (dancing girl press, Fall 2016). She lives in Maine.

Wishbone

By Emile DeWeaver

We play
chicken where the brave
stay the course. Frames will twist,

wrap each other in fuck-mad
embrace. No, not
play—too old, too

practical, for games.
We speed each toward
the other, hearts pecking holes

in our chest. She's gonna
drive through my windshield.
Or, or, or

I've driven this long: clouds
hail self-delusions and wishbones
and nothing's left/right

for us but greasy thoughts
while I'm not-playing
chicken with myself, mad-dogging

the end of the dot-dot
yellow line. Elsewhere she
parasails [insert horizon]. Mash gas

pedal; RPMs shake
me till my lines blur
but, but, but

either she's laying
rubber down this highway
and our chassis shall become

one, or I'm sailing down
this hot strip till it's cool, blue
curtains with buzzards thin as pen
strokes slicing the sky. I'm

so, so determined it's cruel, cruel.
Cruel like once upon this future:
if I changed course and put
the curtains in my
side view and drove one
city over, I'd not see her.

And I'd live
with knowing she's
not not not coming

because she wakes daily

deciding that's the life
she can't live without.

So I crash/So I sail.

About the Author

Emile DeWeaver is a columnist for *Easy Street Magazine* and a 2015 Pushcart Award nominee. He is a member of Prison Renaissance, a group of incarcerated artists who through artistic expression experienced a rebirth of the humanity they once lost. These writers, artists, journalists, and stage performers have dedicated their talents breaking the cycles of mass incarceration.

Old Church by the Sea

By Peg Alford Pursell

I hadn't visited the abandoned church by the sea in many years, not since that day with my teenage daughter. She'd reached that age of awkwardness, so painful to see, when people had begun telling her to calm down, to lower her voice, to walk, not run. I'd brought her to this confused Eden, huge boulders in the garden, cold shadows, the infinite space of sun.

Sad jasmine crawled everywhere, even over the dilapidated fence deteriorating as if the weight of the flowers had caused its demise. I'd imagined we would run and play as in a game of tag, like we had when she was younger, as if we were two butterflies in the tall grass.

She wore dark glasses and sat on a stone bench where a white cat lay sleeping. I didn't dare believe she was looking at me behind those lenses. Her chin tilted up, and I decided she was examining the distant countryside: yellow grass spread with repeated cows, the bay a shimmering backdrop of monotony. A quick wind stroked my bare arms and prodded dark clouds across the sky. It began to rain.

We made the long drive home in silence, her earbuds in place, the tinny chords of her music reaching me behind the wheel. We neared the close-by village, where at the street corner, under the overhang of the roof of the grocery mart, a group of five men sat as if hypnotized. My daughter's head abruptly swiveled, stayed fixed in their direction until we made the turn and left them behind.

How the imagination can forge something from a moment!

Here now the burning light of day rested in all its blue brilliance on the remaining stained glass window of the church, miraculously still intact. The sun bleached only the tips of the wild grasses, while closer to Earth darkness churned like sea reeds. Heavy clouds clung to the distant hills speckled with their animals.

Inside the old church it was almost possible to hear what people do to one another. I always think I'll circle around to the exact explanation for what went wrong.

Having and wanting at the same time, that's what it was to carry my daughter inside me. After, I was emptier than I could ever have imagined, I thought then. Then, when I thought I would have the chance to tell her one day.

About the Author

Peg Alford Pursell is the author of the forthcoming book of stories, *Show Her a Flower, a Bird, a Shadow*. Her work has been published in or forthcoming from *VOLT, RHINO, the Journal of Compressed Creative Arts*, among others, and shortlisted for the Flannery O'Connor Award. She curates *Why There Are Words*, a reading series she founded six years ago in Sausalito, and is the founding editor of WTAW Press, an independent publisher of exceptional literary books. You can find her online at www.pegalfordpursell.com.

Pangea

By Sharon Coleman

Before radiation conjoined continents. In those windy days by the Pacific, when we went to empty our hands of grades, bills, unpaid work. We stood separate. Cold, a cherished forgetting. Something immense. Something distant. We held our smallness in check. We held hands, maybe. Maybe not. I walked in circles around beaches and hills. Thought of a last name of my migrant ancestors I might take if we marry. You stood with the vision of waves.

When contaminated clouds circled our planet, my nephew touched a rain puddle for the first time. He looked into it: his face? You stood. I walked in circles. Rain came down. Milk was measured. Scientists bartered plausible pathologies for wave-swept birds. I told my nephew's parents to take him in. They laughed as he splashed his watery likeness.

We held hands, maybe, and walked inside.

At night it was almost Eden. Nothing more to desire, not even knowledge because *that* we almost had. We became both continent and sea. Now a motorcycle from Japan washes up on shore. I close my eyes, and a seal with the last name of my ancestors swims by. Radiation burns across its body. I didn't take that name. I didn't take yours. In this bed though, we don't practice being together because we are.

Spinning Vinyl

By Sharon Coleman

she shed words like her sister's hand-me-down anger   a mis-sewn dress
she folded into slow july streams, tall dry grasses   over warm granite
of a coast they were moved up and down   too many times   she slept
where the first story   was hammered into the second   across
a threshold nailed shut   the new music of those years
was sadder than the old   she'd sit in her grandmother's wooden chair
mouth words   blackberry thorns   ripe fig's skin   raw lemon
she sat spine straight   in those years the muscles inside
her thighs grew taut   stomach toughened   contour awoke in her face

*

she held the needle over a spinning record   poised to scratch or play
she re-played mustard jars her sister threw, and butter knives   against
another new home   as old as it was   her sister tried to settle
sanded the floors of the first story   the second hovered beyond them
when the stone fireplace grew to the ceiling   *her sister walked into flames*
their father pulled her out   *long hair smoldering*   *small flames*
at the edges of her blouse   wetness straightened waves of their hair
the sisters took turns   on the kitchen stool   their mother took
a long comb, pointed scissors   evened them out in ways her mother could

*

in those years radios buzzed flat seventies' songs   lodged like fallout
at the back of her throat   records her sister had brought home, left
when her sister left   she listened to coastal winds that coursed through
a gap in the hills, eddied in her ears   she pulled her hair
down over them   over warm cave walls   vibrating bone
she took to music older than grandmother's wooden chair   her mother
hummed notes simply   without words   cut squash and tomatoes
took out mozart and satie   whose flaking covers smelled of acid and earth
whose music wrapped in patterns   her spine branched into sound

*

she moved her bed and unread books   books her sister sent
to the story above   a crate of old music stashed behind
her grandmother's chair   she sat   away from the geiger counters of men
and their songs   muscles broadened over the back of her ribs
her cheeks drew back to their framework   the house below grew
distant, quieter anger   september weeds folded into dust   sand
loosened clay-lined soil   she deepened creases in the spines of old books
she began in chalk   continued in pencil   she hummed to words
ocean wind   buckling threshold   spirit fire   over the spinning vinyl

About the Author

Sharon Coleman's a fifth-generation Northern Californian with a penchant for languages and their entangled word roots. She writes for *Poetry Flash*, co-curates the reading series *Lyrics & Dirges* and co-directs the Berkeley Poetry Festival. She the author of a chapbook of poetry, *Half Circle*, and a book of microfiction, *Paris Blinks* (Paper Press, 2016).

Sea

By João Anzanello Carrascoza
Translated by Ilze Duarte

violent, the water crashes, and the white foam advances toward the sand and, eyes stung by the salt, his lips part and he laughs, my boy, and soon another wave builds up, grows and gets ready and *catch this one, Dad*, and we go, side by side, the liquid impact on our bodies, and he laughs again, on his small yellow board, my boy, and the sun sprawls through the spaces, an airplane pierces the sky with the banner Protect your skin with Sundown behind it, and the two of us, lined up, once more, the voluminous wave, he gets in step and catches it on the ascent, and glides on it, aerial fish in revolution, and there he goes, carried away, my boy, and I turn to the beach and see him, laughing, his face like the bow of a sailboat, and over his shoulders the colorful umbrellas, the children with their buoys and their toys, people ambling from one end to the other, and the vendors dragging their carts across the sand, *Ice-cold yerba mate! Cashew nuts, sir? Corn on the corn, corn on the cob*, behind me the open sea, from where the waves are released, *Dad, Dad*, and a big one comes and jolts me, I in a whirl, and he is amused by my carelessness, the incessant waters, waves turning into waves, the murmur of the ocean, the murmur, and the two of us, the two of us, bathed by the same instant (an imperceptible joy), the water, violent, a jet ski tearing the blue surface before us, splat, the white foam moves forward, slaps the sand, eyes stung by the salt, his lips part and he laughs, and I, *close your mouth so you won't take in water*, my boy, and that back-and-forth and forth-and-back, the ebb of minutes we do not notice are passing forever, the minutes so full and so soon dispelled like the foam, and after a pause, *awesome, it was awesome*, the breeze soothes the fever of our bronzed skin, and the commentary in the shade, I and he in the aluminum chairs, the stickiness of the ice cream, *I want a chocolate ice cream bar, Dad*, his hair running across my eyes thirsty to see him smile, and along comes a woman selling fried shrimp on a stick, *No, thank you*, and soon the old man with a trash bag, *May I take the empty cans?*, the warm taste of summer, minimal rest, because he, *let's go, Dad, let's go*, tireless, as if discovering his element, the sea, the sea, the sea that calls, the mugginess burning us silently, slices of me in him, and again, and once more, and another wave, *that one's good, Dad,* and there he goes, the water passes like a heavy bird over our heads, *ah, I couldn't, it broke before I could get there*, and something catches my eye, a young woman dives in and emerges through the foam, Venus born before me, *too bad*, she doesn't fit my moment, the sea, the murmur of the surf, the sounds that break out from the shore, and I see him, he is coming back, positioning himself for the maneuver, clumsy, my boy, in the trepidation of the first lessons, so much sea still ahead, and there, in the shallow water, a couple plays frescobol, the sound of the ball on one racket, tock, on the other, tock, *Come on,* tock, tock, and then the ball dropping in the fluffy silence of the sand, and another airplane, *Skol, the beer that goes down smooth*, and again the wall of water that builds up and, violent, crashes on us, and I look for him among the other bathers, nowhere to be seen, nowhere, and then I refocus in the same direction and, there, suddenly, his face beams, and I recognize myself in him, in the water where he is a part of me, and the moment compels me to smile, maybe this way he will notice—and years later will understand—that happiness is only happiness in that it is finite, I hear the lifeguard's whistle, and that to enjoy it is to be together, even amidst the muddled voices, in our deaf secrets, the undertow, we didn't even notice, it pushed us several yards ahead, over there the **Danger** sign, and I warn him, *That way, Son, that way*, and we move, slow, we move, the weight of the water halting our thighs, and soon we're as light as before, the vigilance dissipates, and he is having fun, and with renewed resolve, he catches the wave a bit too late for the drop, and, gloogloogloogloo, wipes out, *hahahaha,* he running to retrieve his board, and I repeat, *close your mouth so you won't take in water*, and my eyes sting because of the salt, and I see over there another father-and-son, just like us, the two getting wet of each other, this one of that one, that one of this one, different waters from the same sea, the sea, its blue in the blue that is lacking in us, the salt, Dad, where does it come from? *the salt, Son, is made of the sea and makes the sea what it is*, the sea, the substances in the in-and-out of bodies, and I know there is sweet in it coming from me, as there is bitter, and, thus,

we leap into the light of many other summers ahead, the molting of dreams, and everything and nothing changed, and he silent, the sand falls down the hourglass, grain by grain, making what is great, flowing into the quiet, and the twists and turns, the welcomed ones and the resented ones, the cliffs, the unexpected rain showers, the nights of flowing and the days of ebbing, and I, unawares, some gray hair already, in the splash of years renewed, *Wow, how big he's got!*, my boy, such long arms, the earring on his ear, the tattoo on his leg, his surf board long, black, the board of a pro, God, how much we learn and how much we don't even notice while life, life, only a few stretches covered, from one beach to the next, from the hairless face, the water, the white foam, to the shadow on his face, the hairs that poke through the skin, the sun solidifying the day that dawns, the sun that dries the placenta, and yes, suddenly I see the man, he bigger than I, and so many things have we gone through together, to be at hand, things that stuck to our skins like birth marks, the signs of what we are, like the leaf on a palm tree is the palm tree in leaf form, this nose just like that nose, the hands so alike, the voice, *Father*, vigorous, an echo escapes from my lips, *Son*, the molecules blend together, memories fluctuate, one on top of another, a tube, a drop, he lying on his stomach, the comfort of hearing the sounds he made in his room, as if I didn't need him or he me, both of us pretending the sea has no end, and the world is reborn every morning, the world, awake, vast, with its buried treasures and unreachable islands, and between the two of us, between two people, between all of us, always a sea to cross, and in the excitement of it, Pedro, Paulo, Tiago, his friends, *we're going down to the beach, Dad,* and I, *when will you be back?*, the car engine on, the boards on the car top, *Sunday!*, the whistle, like the other times, so young, the sea is theirs now, time to enjoy its waves, to savor unwittingly the taste of the elemental water, to discover the capes, the bays, the promontories, the sand banks, the submerged continents, time to ignore the lighthouses, the signals of the surf, the smell of the breeze, we are what we are, *catch that one, Dad*, the children with their buckets, **from dust we came and to dust we return, life was born of the primeval sea,** the sea belongs to them more than to me, sail away, sail away, because all that is left for me is to float, I already know, the suspicions, I each day farther away into the sea, I know when the undertow pulls even before I get wet, the **Danger** sign, the wave that gets nearer, the strength that drains away, what comes further ahead, I know, the suspicions, the ultimate wave, the mystery that awaits me, the natural anchoring, and the hours come, and the wait doesn't matter, the sand comes, the ringtone of the cell phone, *hello*, the news, and I can imagine how it all happened, the water, violent, the water crashes, violent, the water crashes, and the white foam advances, glooglooglooglooglooo, my eyes stinging with salt, *close your mouth so you won't take in water*, and silence now hovers over me, and I see his lips closed, my boy, forever, there in the sea, in the sea, in the depths of me, and another wave and another wave, the salt stinging my eyes, the salt, the salt

About the Author

João Anzanello Carrascoza is an award-winning writer and professor at the University of São Paulo's School of Communication and Arts. He is the author of the novels *Notebook of a Missing Person* and *At 7 and At 40*, and the short-story collections *The Volume of Silence*, *Thorns and Pins*, and *Small Loves*. His work has been translated into Croatian, French, Italian, Spanish, and Swedish. English translations of his short stories have appeared in *Words Without Borders* and *Granta*.

About the Translator

Ilze Duarte translates works by contemporary Brazilian authors and writes short stories of her own. She lives with her husband and two daughters in Milpitas, California. "Sea" is her first published literary translation.

Frank Vega: It's What's on the Outside That Counts

By Rajpreet Heir

In the outskirts of Boystown, a neighborhood known as Chicago's premier gay district, is a male dance lounge called the Lucky Horseshoe. Within walking distance of the lounge are a sushi restaurant, costume store, nightclub, and large rainbow flags. Inside the near totally dark doorway of the Lucky Horseshoe is an illuminated picture of a shirtless man. The icy cold twenty-four-year-old bar smells of latex and expired cleaning products. The nineties techno is so loud that its pulses can be felt on hard surfaces. The music seems too ambitious, mostly underlining the low energy of Monday night's customers. Eight of them sit in small groups around the huge wooden horseshoe-shaped bar. On the back wall, a large TV is turned to the evening news, and it streaks the mirrors and customers' bottles with neon.

In the center of the bar, Frank Vega dances on an elevated six-by-six rainbow-colored platform. Wearing nothing but combat boots and a black G-string with gold studs down the front, Frank, 5'8" and fifty-six years old, lowers to do the splits. Frank's muscular form, olive-toned skin (save for Speedo tan lines), lack of wrinkles, and flexibility make him seem as if he's in his mid-thirties. Frank has been stripping for twenty-eight years.

Sliding his legs underneath himself until he's kneeling, he tilts his torso back, and allowing just his fingertips to graze the platform, he rhythmically humps the air. As if answering his humps, an African American stripper wearing a knit SpongeBob hat and white G-string leaps on top of the bar, also dancing.

"Is that SpongeBob?" Frank yells, stepping with the music.

"But without the square pants," the stripper yells back. As Frank pivots, hips leading the way, he throws his head back, laughing. His laugh, which comes from low in his stomach, is loud enough to be heard over the stools scraping tile in the back bar and the murmured customer conversation. It's a laugh that endures no obstacles of release from his chest, and even more, it asserts his comfort and knowledge that he is the star of the bar. The laugh, which fills all four corners of the room, boldly imposes his personality, and erases all other dancers, thoughts, and sounds.

Right after Frank finishes his fifteen-minute set and exits the platform, his forehead glowing with perspiration, a thicker white male with a life-size tattoo of a rosary on his chest replaces him, dancing to another techno hit from the predetermined playlist. SpongeBob hops down from the bar and sips at his mixed drink through two straws. Across the room, a giggling dancer towels another dancer as they race into the locker room. The manager doesn't seem to mind that they've left the floor, but he would mind on a Friday or Saturday night, when the lounge typically has over fifty customers. On the weekends, customers stand three deep at the bar and nearly overflow onto the dancing platform.

Frank, dollar bills jammed in his crack and stuck under his waistband, moves around a few new customers and strolls toward the bar. His head is shaved except for a black patch of hair at the center of his hairline, making him look, in his own words, like a Kewpie doll. Frank is thick-legged and burly-chested, and his beard stubble and rich skin color give his face a seasoned look. His voluptuous mouth is full of bright white teeth. Altogether, his features and alert hazel eyes have the zingy look of someone who is on the verge of telling a funny story. With his hand on his hip, Frank unconsciously rubs a sculpted butt cheek—a gesture that seems slightly crude until one realizes humans probably do this all the time, just usually when they are wearing pants.

Two padded faux-leather barstools away from Frank and in the corner, is a middle-aged, stiff-jointed man with a Marines hat pulled low over his face. The man's torso is turned toward Frank rather than the dancer at the center of the room.

In reference to the upbeat seventies song that is playing, Frank, showing his teeth, says, "A guy made a joke earlier that I was dancing when that song came out. I said, 'No I was in monastery school studying to be a priest then.'" He speaks in an amused way, and without confusion or insecurity.

Frank, born and raised in Chicago, comes from a religious family. His parents, of Mexican and Spanish descent, have never been accepting of his career. They send him crazy Easter and Christmas cards saying "God vomits out the lukewarm" and "You're going to Hell … Happy Christmas." When Frank divorced his wife after seven years of marriage, his mother made sure he remembered that divorce is against the Catholic Church. "She'll condemn you to Hell with a big smile on her face," Frank explains, keeping his humorous tone. But briefly, he lowers his head, and then raises it before a nearby customer has even finished taking a swig of beer.

The man in the Marines hat leans forward and offers to buy Frank a drink and Frank accepts, but not in an overtly friendly way, rather in cordial agreement. Being straight, Frank keeps his distance from customers and even has hiding spots in the lounge. He's always aware of space so he can counter the movements of people nearing him.

"People assume I'm gay and I don't feel like arguing. I let them assume what they assume. I've always kept my life and age private," he explains. He first started dancing when he was married, but kept it a secret from acquaintances. He's realized that people see him as a gateway if they're interested in hiring an escort and that they think strippers do drugs and participate in crazy sexual acts with their partners.

"I got into this for dance," he says, abruptly changing his tone. Sassily he places his hands on his hips and looks up as if he's sung a final note and actors in glittery costumes are doing jazz hands behind him. With his head held high and back, he reveals the rounded tip of his wide nose and big nostrils, a commanding nose.

Frank has not always worked for the Lucky Horseshoe; he first started out as a hip-hop dancer, moved on to go-go dancing, opened at the Lucky Horseshoe in 1989, left to work for a club with male and female strippers, acted at Navy Pier, worked for an agency until 2007, and then came back to the Lucky Horseshoe.

He's never had a "man crush" on anyone he has ever worked with, thinks of himself as 100 percent straight and even finds it physically impossible to be with a man; he feels like vomiting. Some straight dancers do try to experiment, as the lounge is the ultimate forgiving ground. According to Frank, almost half of the dancers are straight right now, which is unusual, and most likely because the dance manager is into straight gym guys. Straight dancers realize they can't make much money at co-ed clubs.

"Guys do those jobs because they can sleep with the dancers. The female dancers would say, 'You got me all wet, when are we going to have sex? I want it now.' And *wham bam*, we'd do it in the parking lot. It's not business, it's just pleasure."

The bartender unconsciously licks his lips and runs a hand through his fluffy blond hair as he arrives with Frank's Bud Light. He leans in to tell Frank something and Frank holds up a hand, and says, "Shut *up*!" The bartender looks pleased with himself and as if he wants to stay and talk longer, but Frank turns away. Frank has never been intimate with a man, though he admits that if there ever were a place to experiment, it would be here. However, being straight and giving the illusion of unattainability earns him tips at the Lucky Horseshoe.

"I create a beard," he says, pretending to pull at a long imaginary beard. "Like, a gay guy can create one if he pretends he has a girlfriend so people think he's straight. If a dancer wants popularity, they have to create a beard."

Frank doesn't act like he wants a tip; he doesn't feign interests or stroke customers' egos, and this makes him alluring. If a customer asks why Frank is talking to another customer, he'll tell them, "He's been giving me twenties all night." One time, an enamored, or perhaps competitive, customer told Frank he'd pay him $500 a month *not* to hang out with another customer. Dancers notice after a while that Frank never gives lap dances and it's because he knows he has to really sell them. Most customers don't enter the bar thinking they will spend twenty dollars.

When Frank is hit on by men he tries to gross them out by saying things like: "Blood and diarrhea are a great lubricant for sex!" or "I'm always running on full!" If they ask about the black cock ring he wears around his wrist, he'll say it has sentimental value because it was his dad's.

"Last week a guy said 'I want you inside of me so bad.' I always try to reply with something noncommittal like 'Hell yeah!' or 'A'ight,'" Frank says. Even though Frank considers himself an anti-social stripper, he has accumulated a fan base over the years and when longtime fans come back to the Lucky Horseshoe, they are often amazed how he hasn't aged; his friends call him Dorian Gray.

"You're an old relic," a stripper wearing bandanas on his knees and around his nether regions says in passing. Frank playfully hits his shoulder before he prances away. On the bandanas, Frank says, "They look dumb. He's from a small town in Indiana though. He really likes his job and travels to get here."

After the rosary man finishes his fourth song and as a new dancer wearing assless briefs takes the stage, the man in the Marines hat sucks on the mouth of his empty bottle of beer. More people enter, bringing the total to around fifteen, including those in the back bar.

When the bar first opened, it mostly attracted old men. "If they didn't look eighty, they were eighty."

Over the years, the Lucky Horseshoe has only had one competitor, Madrigals, and they had a pole. "Poles are illogical though and nasty. If a guy shakes the bar between his ass cheeks, he gets fecal juice all over it," Frank says in disgust.

Frank continues to discuss the clientele, specifically mentioning one of the most bizarre clients he has seen in his dancing career: the Quarter Queen. He would fill dancers' G-strings with as many quarters as they could hold. Frank wore a stretchy jock strap and managed to fit eighty dollars in quarters.

"Frank also swings off those chandeliers," a buck-toothed admirer cuts in, nodding his head upwards. Four large dusty chandeliers with glass beads hang across the bar's ceiling.

"Those things are ready to fall," Frank replies and then turns his broad back on him and the young man moves on.

Frank leaves his beer and walks around the corner to the locker room. The dusty floor in the locker room resembles a warehouse floor and since a ceiling is absent, large pipes are visible. Against one wall is a set of wooden lockers that a bartender made himself. The lockers are necessary because any money lying out, even in a backpack, can be stolen. Frank knows someone that set $200 down on top of the lockers once and after he returned from helping someone move boxes, the money was gone. "You never know what people need money for," he says, his voice trailing off. Aside from his friendship with Robby, a stripper around his own age, Frank rarely gets personal with other dancers; his relationships with them are surface level and based on joking around.

Passing the lockers, Frank steps into a small bathroom, and then he points out the pile of baby powder in front of the toilet. Frank steps on the baby powder before going out to dance to ensure he won't slip on the stage. Even in combat boots, the stage can be slippery if it's smeared with sweat or if someone spills a drink on it. Pretending to take little steps, his junk jiggling with the movement, he says, "I leave white footprints everywhere."

Further into the locker room are a few stripper policy sheets taped to a wall. One is unofficially known as the Frank Vega Rule. One night, Frank made out with a woman and she kept buying him drinks. The owner didn't yell, but instead printed a sign that says: "This is a gay bar, no making out with women." Under Frank's rule is another policy known as the Nathan Rule: "You can't finger-bang a girl, but finger-banging a guy is okay." There used to be a rule that dancers had to remove their clothing within forty-five seconds, making the men into go-go dancers. The manager's fear was that if people came in the door and saw someone dancing with their clothes on, they would leave.

Next to the policy wall are large shelves with boxes of supplies, and another room with a few benches and a muscular stripper flipping through a magazine. His feet are in running shoes. "Have you explained shelf life?" he asks.

"The manager sent out a message about stripper shelf life and now the dancers say I've used mine up," Frank explains and laughs, seemingly unaffected. He claims he's doing better now with fans than he ever has. The dancers have to reaudition quarterly and at his most recent audition, the audience gave Frank, and only Frank, a standing ovation. The manager told him to get off the stage and he didn't even have to dance. And despite having used up his shelf life, Frank says he is in great shape physically.

"I know twenty-year olds with knee pain. They jump off stage, but I don't, I *glide off*," he says, winging his arms out and dramatically gliding a few feet to the left. Recently, he saw a young dancer fall on his back after attempting a handstand.

"I was like, "Are you okay? You almost just died!" Frank says, widening his eyes and inflecting his voice. "The dancer had so much pride and pretended he was fine," Frank says, laughing, and in an instant, he turns stern—his mouth set and eyes unblinking. "Handstands aren't sexy anyways. It's not dancing."

After leaving the locker room, a dancer approaches Frank and tells him he has to have a shot with the manager since it's the manager's birthday. Seeing Frank's hesitation, the dancer tells him, "At least it's cinnamon. It'll clean out your sinuses."

When Frank returns and goes back to stand at the bar, he says he's worried about being hungover on his day off. On his days off, Frank doesn't like to drink or go clubbing because he's usually partied out and, since he dances erotically for hours each week, he's forgotten how to dance normally.

Instead, Frank divides his time by working out, acting class, open mics, and going to the movies. Sometimes he goes and watches three at a time. Frank got hooked to the film industry when he was nineteen and walking home from work. He saw a crew shooting Michael Mann's *Thief* and conned his way into being an extra. Working for hours in the cold and the rain did not bother Frank, and when filming concluded at 2 AM, everyone received steak dinners off a truck, leading Frank to decide he had found his passion. He quit his catering job and went to a nearby college to study Drama, but dropped out after his first year when he realized the difficult path of actors.

"I don't regret it. Drama school majors don't usually end up acting anyway and I didn't like how they are all about preparing you for rejection," he says.

Frank's only child, a twenty-six-year-old son from his past marriage, does not share the same interests, and instead is studying to become a physical therapist. Frank never wanted children, but five years into their marriage, his ex-wife kept bothering him about a baby so he "did her a favor" and let her get pregnant. A few years after his son was born, they divorced and his in-laws, who never liked Frank, decided that if Frank got involved, their monetary support for Frank's son would end.

The son will say, "Now you want to know about me" if Frank tries to talk to him, so instead they talk about random stuff like Taco Bell for an hour. Frank used to get phone calls and a card for Father's Day, but it's all stopped.

"It's up to him if we will become closer," Frank says, rubbing his large elbow. Even this most banal of gestures attracts the worshipful gaze of a paste-complexioned patron on the other side of the bar. "It doesn't bother me. I can see everyone's view."

"My butt is so sore," mutters a dancer in yellow briefs who is kneeling on a nearby barstool and swiveling side to side. Though he appears to be talking to himself, Frank shifts his attention to him. This dancer is new and has already switched his name three times in the past few weeks. "Tristan, Miguel, nice to meet you ... again," Frank laughs, snap-happy once more. "Once he was Tucker—what a weird name." Frank never uses stage names because he forgets what he picked. Another part of being new is learning to avoid customers who won't tip.

"A new dancer will come up to me and say that a guy only tipped him a dollar and he shoved a finger up his ass. I'll say you're lucky it wasn't two dollars and he didn't shove two fingers up your ass," Frank says through more belly laughs. New guys also try cock rings, which tie off erections and stop blood flow, and "generally push things to the front."

"You can do it at work, but then the next guy might have the same thing too," Frank says, pushing around the coaster in front of him. Frank knows one guy that can't have sex with his boyfriend now without one. Dancers are known to take Viagra before their shift. "Maybe if you're making $500 a night that makes sense, but most end up spending more on the Viagra," Frank explains.

A man and woman enter the bar and then turn around and leave, the woman with her hands on her hips. Female customers are often Frank's least favorite. Once a woman came in with her three gay guy friends and seemed to be peeved by the environment.

"She takes out a dollar, slams it down, and yells for me, 'put a shirt on!'" Frank, forever under a roving spotlight says, imitating her movements, slamming his own hand down, cock ring sliding on his wrist. "She did this two more times and then I tore the dollars into confetti and sprinkled it over her."

Women aren't good customers typically because they tend to get a mob mentality, they don't tip, they turn off other customers, and they want to be the show. However, Frank sometimes gets women to lie on the bar and he goes in between their legs and kisses their necks. People scream, the woman likes it, and Frank enjoys himself too. That's how Frank met his current girlfriend. She came in with gay friends and one of the friends said he knew Frank was straight because he hadn't looked at him the whole night. "My girlfriend visits me at work sometimes," he says and then pauses. "She doesn't love that I dance with other women, but she understands they come in." He thinks people stereotype him as a player because of his looks. In his opinion, he's shy around women and an evolved male because of his past romantic failures.

Suddenly, Frank begins describing the funniest thing he's seen at the lounge recently: a guy with the deflated brown skin of his ball hanging out, "like shit." Frank says, "There's no such thing as a wardrobe malfunction here. He knew it was out—it was purposeful." Later the stripper asked Frank if he looked good and Frank told him it looked like shit was dangling from his crack.

Shaggy's "It Wasn't Me" starts and the dancer with the SpongeBob hat says to a customer, "He was bad at cheating." The bartender moves around behind the bar, lazily passing customers and removing empty bottles. Frank turns when the manager taps him on the shoulder. The two look at a clipboard under the glow of the manager's phone and Frank says, "You're right, I did forget to dance!" However, Frank doesn't seem ruffled, nor does the manager. Management doesn't seem to be spandex-tight with rule enforcement.

"Some guys could dance all fucking night," Frank states. In fact, as the stripper on stage drops to do a one-armed push-up, two other dancers start moving with the music several feet away. Another in red Adidas underwear climbs up on the bar.

Looking at his watch, Frank massages his elbow again and starts to move to the back bar to dance his set. The platform in the back bar is made up of eighteen green, red, and yellow squares. Surrounding the platform are a bunch of clear plastic chairs and small tables, and they change color every few seconds due to the disco light.

Once in one of those chairs, Frank says he saw a short stripper with dreads doing an intimate handstand as part of a lap dance for an eighty-year-old man. The dancer had "Billy" tattooed on one ass cheek, and Frank joked he got the first half of the tattoo removed because it said "Hill."

As a Rihanna song starts, Frank steps onto the stage and begins marching with the music, both hands bent at the wrist. A young man in a T-shirt sits in the far back corner. An elderly man emerges and goes straight to Frank to shove a few bills under his waistband. Frank tilts his head and mouths, "Thank you." Frank's smile is saturated in appreciation, as if the man had offered to fix his car, clean his gutters, or cater his Christmas party for free.

Frank turns to start dancing again and soon after the next song starts, another older man walks up to the platform. Frank looks the man up and down: the scuffed tennis shoes, his wrinkled khakis, his polo, his tousled hair; his warm worshipful breaths. Frank seems to recognize him, and he sinks slowly, butterflying his knees out, and hugs the man, gently pressing the man's face to his downy chest. The hug seems more kind than sensual, like the sort of hug a middle school counselor gives to a student when they meet again years later, when the student can finally look people in the eye—a hug of tenderness and continued acceptance. Yet the two are definitely not equals.

A time Frank truly felt his dancing was more of an outreach was when he was paid to dance at an "old people's home where people were older than old and had $200 in singles." Some old men came forward and told him they had been in the closet their whole lives.

The newcomer takes a seat on the same side of the room as the man in the corner. A fast pop song plays: "Tonight is your lucky night/I know you want it." Frank dances toward the men and abruptly crumples to the ground in a display of absolutely wounded masculinity, his face in anguish, his body laid out flat, and his arms next to his sides. "Yeah Frank!" yells a hairless dancer striding past. The music seems louder than usual.

From his dramatically splayed position, he lifts his legs directly above himself and opens them gradually, bringing dawn into the room a few degrees at a time. His audience seems to be holding its breath, in case Frank or all the Lucky Horseshoe might tip into Lake Michigan; any misstep will cause friendly fire. Sensing the energy emanating from the platform, another customer draws toward the huge side window overlooking the action and peers in, clutching his beer tightly. He stares the skin off Frank.

Frank, at this point, is a hypnotic force. He's more powerful now than when he stands at the bar. Face to face, it's easy to admire his tan, muscles, and high-voltage mannerisms, but regular interactions do not convey his verve, his vigor on the dancing platform. Master of his form on the stage, he simultaneously radiates coolness and an American ease.

Frank slides himself up and bends forward to sit on his knees, and then he pumps his arms forward. The next song starts and Frank sweeps diagonally across the platform, cutting his hands through the air in fast arcs, and plunges through rigidly sexy steps. Marching and turning, marching and turning with animal rhythm and a relaxed expression, he seems even fuller of a person now that he's absorbed his audiences' wistfulness.

Later, when the room has grinded back to normal, Frank, moving with big steps, reappears flushed and seeming larger than before he danced, as if he's knocked his enemy out with one punch. Pow. Suddenly, next to a large boxing video game machine, cider ad, and shelf containing *Windy City* magazine, *BOI* magazine, and gay pride brochures, he is very tall and very close.

He says, "I'm pretty freaky, athletically. I never took dance classes. When I dance, nothing limits me."

A black man in his forties wearing denim shorts and a sleeveless cotton shirt hovers behind Frank until Frank turns and gives him a big hug. It's odd to see Frank truly excited to hug another man; Frank's eyes are even closed. This is someone who does not clutter Frank's space.

Robby, another dancer, and a "big time gay," and a "giant gay whore," is Frank's best friend. Frank loves watching Robby perform because he is cheerful, outgoing, and openly sexual. Plus, no one is as selfless about tipping as Robby; when Robby finds a customer who pays in twenties, he lets Frank know. Robby is especially good at getting twenties because he'll ask customers, "Can I have that twenty?"

Frank says he and Robby are complete opposites, because outside of the lounge, Robby is the exact same. If the two are walking down the street, Robby will interrupt Frank to ogle and whistle at men they pass, as "He just wants to get laid." Before working at the lounge, Frank had never had a best friend or even been close to a fellow dancer.

Frank isn't sure he's Robby's best friend. The two go to a diner after work sometimes, but Robby always has to leave to escort or do a private show. Frank claims Robby appreciates his sentiment though. Every two months, Frank starts crying while drinking and confesses to Robby that he's never met someone so honest and Robby will say, "Okay Frank, I know you mean it."

Now Frank's arm is around Robby and the two unlikely friends turn to study the clipboard. With Robby's extra layers—shorts, a shirt, and sandals—and with Frank's bare torso, muscular or not, Frank appears vulnerable. Skin suddenly is what it is: just a thin organ protecting a body. Similar to the customers Frank has had today, Frank's gaze is somewhat tender and timid, as if he's afraid Robby might pivot too fast and disappear. Frank doesn't think Robby's homosexuality even comes into play with their friendship, but in this place of in-between-ness, the stretched smile on Frank's face almost seems pleading.

About the Author

Rajpreet lives near Washington, DC, and is a third-year in George Mason University's MFA program, where she is the sole recipient of the 2015-2016 Nonfiction Thesis Fellowship. Her work has been published by *The Normal School*, *Aunt Lute Books*, *Apogee*, and *Indianapolis Woman Magazine*.

Veils

By Gray Tolhurst

bridge to bring the language together

(Babylon)

divided the channels

(woven)

you can just as well do the one thing as the other,
that is to say where my reason and reflection say:
you cannot act and yet here is where I have to act
to act upon faith but reflection has closed the road
cannot do otherwise because I am a reflection

festival of aerial crossings

the world without memory

a disappearance of bodies

(a component of the body

like any other
                        living dust
light-signals

to hear voices

identical days

all feeling optical

psychic homeland

the territorial body

oscillating

I feel a moon within me
same bay as in the eyes
curve of glass floating
to the sky my hand grazes it
it is not a facsimile
of this worried field
lights in the pale ashes of eyes
as if they could hold a form such as my own in their water

I become inherited
I fill her blood with my own
even names collapse and form
burial grounds

lay your hand off it
relax control of what little is given
simply speak, it is enough for now

(Three Photographs)

we were in the dry lakebed

tools had become just shape

sky water knit by trees

•

doubt creeps in

somehow it is like smoke

the evidence of a death

•

heaped under white sky

each house already a ruin

built like that

from *Topographies*

a bridge into the sky

(interrupted)

museum of glass structures

the interior of the piano

each note an element

the root of a sun

sidereal woman is the house

the hardwood floor I am

within it a glass of wine

swimming

how couldn't we

the room a plain room

a pale yellow organ

color blooms into objects

the flash of a bulb beneath a door

crucified on the lawn a red star

a decaying alphabet

the Haunted West

spot-lit as if a set

lost among the flowers

blues as ghost music

I hear it from beyond

train cutting the town in two

a vibrating glass speaking

in two the room bisected

my grandmother amongst glass animals

landscape of bones and rusted stoves

skeleton of a dog complete

twinned in others

the sea stuck in my eyes

About the Author

Gray Tolhurst is currently based in San Francisco, CA where he lives in an old convent. He holds an MA in creative writing from San Francisco State University where he was the art editor of *Fourteen Hills Literary Review*. His poems have appeared in *Comma Poetry*, *New American Writing*, and *Switchback*. He is also a musician and plays bass in psychedelic rock band the Coo Coo Birds.

Marshall Levitow

By Han Ong

I call Norton and (where else would a number made available on the internet get you?) speak to a young voice, front-of-office, an unpaid intern probably, not unfriendly, not unhelpful, but the gist is the sooner I get past him, the sooner I'll get to—not exactly the person I wish to speak to; or even the person who would give me the number (or God forbid, the physical whereabouts) of the person I wish to speak to, but— the first in a relay team whose job it is to get me to perform—inasmuch as these things can be done over the phone—my bona fides, a kind of humbling upon humbling, before the information can be surrendered either on that first call (but, as I said, after many transfers) or hours or days later, with an intervening wait that is a further dramatization of how far away I am from the gates. And either way there will come a sigh from the other end that might as well be issuing from my own lips to acknowledge both the picayune quality of this quest ("Hi, I know he no longer works at Norton but this is my last contact point for him?": always that sentence-as-question tone to ingratiate and assuage) and my complete lack of qualification to undertake even such a picayune quest ("I'm his, um, I was his student and I am … I'm compiling notes for his biographer.").

Fifteen or so minutes and four different speakers later (each of whom I imagine to sit successively higher up in the Norton food chain, but really, who can tell?), I am told to call the former secretary of the man I wish to speak to. It's been at least two decades since he was employed here, I'm told. I know, I say. And, well, the reason nobody has any contact info for him—well, actually the last person who would have had it, Valerie, our great copy editor who has been here since the fifties, she just passed away. Well, not *just*, but she passed away. I'm sorry, I say. And also, the real *real* reason nobody has a contact number for him is that he cut himself off from us when he left. There was, um, rancor. Great rancor. A blowout. Cops had to be called. I didn't know, I say. Well, that's the news that's fit to print, the speaker says. So the secretary is … ? I have no idea, the speaker says. We have her number here because she's been longtime friends with the secretary of our publisher, the head honcho. That's why her number's available. I have no idea what you'll find if you call—if she's still alive. But if anyone would know where Marshall Levitow is, it would be her, Cora Lynn would be the one. God, she must be in her eighties by now? Anyway Sarabeth is maybe the same age, and she's still kicking and giving all of us a run for our money. I presume Sarabeth is the publisher's secretary, Cora Lynn's friend, but I don't ask. I say to the speaker: I'm thinking Mr. Levitow is still alive? Because otherwise, a man of his distinction, *The New York Times* would've run an obituary and I haven't been able to find any? You may be right, the speaker says, but again I can't help you there, I don't know if he's dead or alive. He might have fled to Cuba, for all I know. It's a joke but the speaker's tone is mirthless. You know, she says, I'm going to transfer you back to my secretary, and you can leave your contact info with her, and if I can think of any writer we have in-house who used to be edited by Mr. Levitow, although no name is springing to mind right now, which could mean there's nobody who fits that description, but just in case, leave your number and your email and if I can think of a new lead, I'll send it your way. Thank you, I say.

But Cora Lynn Baker is very much alive. Yes I'm Cora Lynn Baker and yes I worked at Norton as Marshall Levitow's secretary, she says to my query. I explain why I'm looking for her former boss and she waits a minute before replying: Well, yes, I remember Mr. Laurence. He passed away, I say. I heard something about that, Cora Lynn says. How old was he? Mid-sixties, I say. That's … that's very young, Cora Lynn says. He killed himself, I say. He took pills. I'm so sorry to hear that, Cora Lynn says. That is a surprise. Why? I say. Why would that be a surprise? The Mr. Laurence I knew, Cora Lynn says, was full of life. Full of fight. Pugnacious, you could say. Did he and Mr. Levitow get into a lot of arguments? Not a lot, Cora Lynn says, but when they did, Mr. Laurence you could hear him from outside the office even with the door closed. He was a tough cookie. I recognize this man, I say. Cora Lynn doesn't say anything else, so I repeat my question: Cora Lynn, do you think I can pay Mr. Levitow a visit? Is he around? Oh, Cora Lynn says, he would like that very much. I don't think he gets much visitors. And I don't think he gets a chance to talk about them old days a lot. Not where he is.

Cora Lynn, eighty-something, dressed up for the occasion: a hat pinned to her wig; a line of white powder visible at the back of the neck so that the wig won't tickle where it comes to rest on skin. Her perfume smells like three different scents: alcohol, suggesting a disinfectant, menthol as in some kind of muscle rub, and above both, an overpowering floral aroma, like a scented candle. She has on sensible flats, black patent leather, with a decorative gold ring near the toes. She has put on shiny nylons, and on her floral-print blouse she has pinned a brooch of a salamander coalescing from red jewels, the red of its eyes darker than the surrounding body. She's as excited/anxious as I am, and when the male nurse wheels Marshall Levitow into our quiet corner of what is referred to as the day room, she stands up immediately, holding onto my hand for support. Hello, Mr. Levitow, do you recognize me? she says.

Cora Lynn! he says. You're a sight for sore eyes.

Ohh, she says flirtatiously. Your eyes are not sore at all.

In the car service, Cora Lynn had told me that Marshall Levitow is younger by at least five years, putting him in his late seventies. Come give me a hug, he says, and she approaches. The male nurse waits until they finish before telling us he'll be back to take Mr. Levitow to the dining room for lunch and that we're welcome to join if we wish.

Who have you brought with you? Levitow says.

I introduce myself. My full name and that I'd been a student of Laurence's.

Oh my God, Levitow says, slapping his knee.

I hope you don't mind, I say. My coming to visit.

Are you kidding? he says.

Cora Lynn sits back down at my side.

I've brought some questions and I also hope you don't mind if I record our conversation.

How are they treating you here, Mr. Levitow? Cora Lynn says.

I wish I could say I can't complain, but I can complain and I do complain. But what are you going to do? Growing old. He shakes his head.

And your health? How is your health? Cora Lynn says.

How is yours, Cora Lynn? You're going to outlive me, Levitow says.

I don't know about that, Cora Lynn says. Today is a good day but tomorrow, who knows?

Well you look good today, that's for sure, Levitow says.

Because I'm coming to see you!

You should come more often.

The truth is, I haven't been getting out of the house too much these days, Cora Lynn says. Thank God for this young man.

Well, thank God, Levitow says. So you say you're going to record this? I don't see a tape recorder.

I'm using my phone, I say. Would that be all right?

That thing records? Levitow says, then laughs. But of course it does. Why am I surprised?

It records audio and video. We'll just do audio.

That's fine with me, Levitow says.

He wants to talk about Mr. Laurence, Cora Lynn says.

It's too bad about Laurence, Levitow says.

May I start by asking you if you were surprised? When you heard— first, how did you hear of it?

It must have been the papers, I guess, Levitow says. I don't know who else could've told me. I don't keep in contact with a lot of people from the book days. It was in the papers, wasn't it?

Yes.

So that is what happened. I read every day. *The New York Times*, mostly. You'd think there'd be a line for it here, and there is—a line and a pecking order, and I guess I've been here going on nine years, so I'm higher up in that order than when I first came, but I had them install a computer, a cheap one, not much bells and whistle, just a screen and the internet, and—listen. Let me ask you. Is fifty bucks a good price for the internet?

Is that what you're paying? Fifty a month?

Does that sound like what it would cost?

Yeah, I say, trying to think of what we pay for the service at Dutch Kills. That sounds reasonable.

Because I don't want to be the kind of person who always thinks he's being taken advantage of, but sometimes you just have to wonder. So I was saying …

The New York Times? Laurence's death?

I keep up with the papers on my computer although Manuel, the nurse, I call him my nurse but he's really everybody's nurse during the day, Manuel, he said he worried that once I had a computer in my room, I wouldn't ever come out again, and he worried that once I made a request for a computer in my room, others would do the same, but that hasn't happened, and I try not to let the first thing happen too much, and besides unless you're sick you have to show up for meals in the dining room and I have my friends here and I like to keep up.

Oh, what do you talk about? Cora Lynn says.

We don't. Not much anyway. Henry he's in a wheelchair like me and Albert, he's ninety, and he's blind, and some days he asks me to describe what the weather's like outside, but we're happy to sit there and look at the others, happy to keep an eye on one another and know that we've made it one more day. Just old friends doing what old friends do.

That makes me happy hearing that, Cora Lynn says.

Were you surprised when you read that Laurence had killed himself? I say.

I can't say I'm surprised by anything much anymore. Sad. Certainly sad. I didn't get to know Laurence very well. We worked on three books together—

His first three, I say.

Yes, the first ones. But in those days, who knows if it's still like this, it wasn't unusual for an editor, at that point I was senior editor and to prove my mettle and my worth I felt, we all did, people hovering near the same rungs, that we needed to acquire and promote and edit as many different voices as we could, to see who would stick. Not that we didn't believe in those we were acquiring, and not that we looked out for quantity over quality, rather that we had to look out for quality *and* quantity. Advances weren't crazy so you could do this. You could publish someone with a not-too-big outlay of money, and so the risk, from the publisher's perspective, you could take this, and we did, over and over. By the time I left the business, it was a whole different game. But this is business talk. You want to know about Laurence. So let's say that ... Um, um ...

You were saying that you didn't get to know Laurence too well.

Ah, yes, thank you, young man. Because I had equal relationships, if you will, with about two dozen other writers that I was also editing, and I tried hard not to play favorites, because writers, well, they can be like children with petty demands that may seem petty on the surface but are usually hiding some bigger test that they're asking you to pass. They are selfish children who have been neglected by their parents and are always looking for surrogates in the larger world. Levitow laughs.

Was Laurence like that?

Oh, they were all like that!

But Laurence in particular?

Not more or less than the others, Levitow says.

When you acquired Laurence's first book, I say, was there a sense of his "voice," if you will, or "style," or "contribution"—

These are good words, go on, Levitow says.

—was there a sense of his take on gay life marking a change from the gay books that were being published at the time?

Let me see, Levitow says.

I wait in vain for an answer, so I prompt him with, I'm trying to figure out what his historical place is in this genre that's called "gay lit."

I liked his voice, Levitow says. His written voice, I mean. I realize that's not sufficient. Let me see ... It's so long ago.

Oh, you can do it, Mr. Levitow, Cora Lynn says. You sound like your mind is as sharp as ever.

Levitow smiles at her. Laurence Warshow, Levitow says. Then repeats the name a few more times, still adding nothing to his recollection. I berate myself for shortsightedness. I should've brought the three books Levitow and Laurence worked on. Should've reread them, marking passages and pages to recite to this old man, who of course would need his memory jogged—a storied career, Laurence Warshow just one strand in it. The Queen of Angels Rest Home in Flushing, Queens. Dark-carpeted "day" room, whose windows face the fenced parking lot, glimmers on the gray water of what the greeter had told us was the Flushing Bay visible beyond denuded trees beyond the parked vans and cars, which includes our car service waiting. There are fake flowers in a large vase parked on the coffee table in front of us, and in another vase on a side table underneath a mirror placed too high for a man in a wheelchair to be able to see himself in. Fallen balloons anchor a corner of the floor in the sitting area opposite ours, the two spaces connected by a windowed walkway floored in parquet. The air smells like Cora Lynn, but I don't know if it's she who's rearranged the chemistry of the atmosphere or if it's just the scent shared by old people wherever you go. Her hands are quivering on her lap. Perhaps she understands that this early in the conversation we've landed on a decisive gap in Levitow's memory. He can't walk, or at least isn't trusted to do so by this establishment and his doctors, and though his speech is sharp, his appearance does not put him at odds with his environment. He has shoulders that dip so low as to make his clavicle look like a frown. Big up top, his legs are sticks, and I wonder if this mismatch is the reason for the wheelchair or the other way around: if absolved of work, the lower half of his body has stopped claiming its share of the food he takes in. His jeans are old looking, so too the long-sleeved plaid shirt, and I can't tell if the spots of shine on them are from too much wear or bad laundering.

Were you impressed, reading that first book, that this was the work of a self-taught man?

Well, I didn't know anything about that. I admired the writing and knowing that he was a self-taught writer added a dimension to my admiration, but only after the fact of having finished the manuscript.

The difficulty I have in answering your question comes from the fact that I didn't have much knowledge of what you call gay literature. Certainly, I knew of Ed Mallory's work. Ed had made such a big splash, a historical splash, because suddenly what they used to call "the love that did not dare speak its name" was, in Ed's book, speaking and describing and explaining. So he deservedly got a lot of attention. When Laurence came along, I would say that the task of attracting attention was much more difficult, because the subject matter was no longer novel. It was already taken for granted that homosexuality could be a legitimate subject matter. So I would say that Laurence's task—not that he would call it that—was much more difficult. And Laurence, the way he made a name for himself, and I can't claim that I understood it then, but I do now, after the fact, long after the fact, is that he had an *assumption*, if you will, that he was going to write for his people, his group of homosexuals, that their lives were worthy of being written about without it being, as with Ed Mallory, a kind of dramatized argument for equal treatment or equal rights. He had an arrogance, Laurence had, and his homosexuals were selfish, ogreish, attitudinous, kind sometimes but almost despite themselves, in other words his were young homosexuals, young in both age and outlook, and I think this was what resonated with the younger critics, both homosexual and heterosexual, the energy of it, the seductiveness of this assumption. And I would say—again, I did not know it at the time, I was attracted to the energy of the book but I couldn't have said more beyond that—I would say that Laurence was the only one of the second generation, Ed being by himself, I would say, in that first generation, but maybe this is not fair? God knows we're not giving people like EM Forster their due, and of course Jimmy Baldwin, and then there's Gore Vidal and Ed White. But as I said, I'm no historian, no expert. But in that generation immediately following Ed Mallory's splash, Laurence was the sole one, or at the very least the first one for the longest time, to leap from Ed's pleading for equal citizenship and to take it for granted that homosexuals did not have to plead.

Levitow is smiling. He is back in his cerebral element, the lapse leapt over. Cora Lynn is looking at me and smiling.

And AIDS?

What about AIDS? Levitow says.

Laurence's work, how did it adapt or respond, do you think?

I don't know that I would characterize his writing as adapting or responding to that. We never talked about the personal toll it took. Or if he himself had a scare. I heard from a younger gay writer, but years later, that he had had some sort of health scare. But I don't know if this was AIDS or some other illness. He was very discreet about these things, and I understand that discreet might be a strange word to describe someone who wrote a racy book—this is his last book with me—but let's say he was more willing to disclose truths about his life in that area than in the area of health.

Do you think he responded to AIDS by ignoring it, by writing a book that was unapologetically sexual?

I don't know if I would say that. The truth would be closer to say that he'd been working on that book for much longer than AIDS had been a presence in his life and in the lives of his friends. Looking back on it, I would say that the first three books shared the same tone. All unapologetic, all celebratory and not mournful. They might have been started if not at the same time, then close to it, and he worked on them simultaneously, going from one to the next, and the order in which they were published reflected the order in which he finished them.

Why did his relationship with you end after three books?

Frankly because his head got too big for his body. Levitow shakes his head. He asked for stupid things!

Like what.

A bigger advance. There was no way we were going to pay what he and his agent asked for. So he, I believe, got it from another publisher, and that book didn't do too well, and so he screwed himself. He was adrift in a house with whom he established an understanding that was strictly commercial, so once he failed to deliver, he only had himself to blame if he was cut adrift. This happens with a lot of writers, don't get me wrong, but Laurence, after three books, needed some other kind of book, some other story, and he wasn't willing to test himself to find that story, and readers began to take him for granted, and rightly so.

Did you have suggestions for him about what this new kind of story might be?

What's the use? By that point, he'd stopped talking to me.

But would you have?

If I did, I don't remember now. But make no mistake, I'm not saying that I'm a master of plot or rather plots. I would've … Let's see—I *might've* counseled him to write more about AIDS. So you're right. I would've said he needed to respond to that. There was readerly interest in what kind of shape AIDS was making in the world of homosexuals and of course in the larger world. And he did write that, eventually. But I think he waited. Because he didn't want to jump from youthful energy to a premature old age. But by the time he wrote about that maybe he was playing catch up with other writers who had taken the bit between their teeth and run with it, who deserved more of the attention.

Did you edit any other gay writers, Mr. Levitow?

One or two others. Wilson Crenshaw and, and, let's see …

Cora Lynn says, Mr. Whitemore?

Thank you, Cora Lynn. Whitemore Harrison. And Wilson Crenshaw.

How would you describe them, relative to Laurence?

Well, Mr. Crenshaw was African-American. Is, I mean is. And he had a take on the subject that included that. And Mr. Harrison, he will tell you outright that he was more indebted to non-homosexual writers. His idols were southern, Flannery O'Connor and Carson McCullers. So though he wrote about homosexual characters, that would not be how he would describe his focus. It's inevitable, the niche is what what-you-call gay literature occupies more and more as the younger generation moves on and becomes more ambitious. But Whitemore, he never once talked about Laurence, and I wouldn't know what he felt about Laurence, either positive or negative.

He wrote a bad review for one of Laurence's later books. In *The New York Times*, I believe.

Maybe Laurence deserved a bad review for one of his later books, Levitow says.

So you weren't aware of any kind of feud?

Everyone feuds, Levitow says. All like children, like I said. In the end, what does it matter? Do people still read Whitemore? Do people still read Laurence? I can't say. I don't keep up with the tastemaking that goes on these days. When I read, I read the news. I read the same handful of people that has piqued my interest from the beginning. Philip Roth, Updike, God bless him, Salinger, God bless him too, Vonnegut, DeLillo, I suppose you could include DeLillo in the bunch. These are the writers I'm interested in.

All white men, I say.

I wouldn't make too much of that, Levitow says.

Cora Lynn looks at me like I've just made bad form. You don't think people read Laurence still?

Levitow shrugs. I suppose that death has returned him momentarily to the spotlight.

I suppose it has.

Is that why there is interest in his biography? Levitow says. To take advantage of the momentary spotlight.

Mr. Levitow, I say, you know how long it takes to write a book. By the time any kind of biographical undertaking is finished, the spotlight would have long moved on.

You may be right, Levitow says. He sighs. Excuse my bitterness. I'm just a bitter old man. I hold no rancor against Laurence. But you have made me relive how angry I was when the negotiations after his third—and might I add, very successful, no small thanks to Norton, to myself, and the countless other hardworking people who made sure that everybody but everybody paid attention to Laurence and his writing—after everything, for things to turn out the way they did, well, Laurence was to blame. Laurence was to blame when he was turned out of the house he joined after Norton. He was to blame for having no one to champion him and to shelter him from the tough commercial times ahead.

Are you saying you would have done that at Norton, even if the books after his third one had not sold as well, had continued not selling?

I am not out to make myself a hero. I'm sure there would've been consequences and I would have been forced to cut him loose. Those were tough times, getting tougher. But I would have fought for him to stick around for far longer. I would have provided counsel. I am not anyone's father, and Laurence might've rejected my advice, but I would have acted as honorably as I could, within reason and within the circumstances. I had writers who we had to cut loose. The command came from on high. I rose to vice president of the company but that did not shield my writers. That did not shield *me*! This is an American business, bottom line. Well, there you have it. Those two words. Bottom line. But we put out good books. Some of them great. Within the constraints, you could say things were more heroic than not. Laurence might still last. As I said, the death might shine a spotlight and in doing so, might remind people of the value of his voice, the contagiousness and the seductiveness of that voice, which, if you want more reminiscence, that voice stands in marked contrast to the person himself, who was ornery, argumentative, and not to assign psychotherapy to my nonexistent skill set, but he gave the impression of fighting to become who he was, and even once he became himself, he was still fighting, he knew no other way. I'm not saying he fought me every step of the way when I was editing his manuscripts. In fact, he was often amenable to, let's say, for example, wholesale transpositions of paragraphs or sections or even chapters. He listened when I explained. He said he would take my comments and suggestions into consideration and I would say he kept most of them. The fight would be, I guess, on word choices, on a certain lack of generosity in his outlook on other people, you know, lightly disguised caricatures of people in our circle, whom I recognized, and this being such a small world, who I knew would be hurt, first off, and would want to take revenge in any way, secondly.

Would you give me an example of some famous person he caricatured that you counseled him against?

I can't remember, Levitow says. I give him a moment, to which he responds: I really can't.

How about an example of word choices that he tangled with you on? I say.

Um, um, I'm sorry, but this is too far back and I can't recall … Let's just say he liked slang, and street words, and he liked to repeat the same words over and over, and I remember saying to him that as a writer it behooved him to work on an expanded vocabulary, and he said, I remember him replying, that he was using repetition as percussion. But as far as I was concerned, a little of that went a long way. Did you bring any of the first three books with you?

I'm afraid I didn't.

Too bad.

I could send them to you and come back in a few weeks, after you've reread them, and maybe we could have a—deeper? A deeper conversation?

That would be good.

If you were me, I say, is there something about Laurence you would ask?

He had the temperament of a child. I know I've said that all writers are children but that is not what I mean. I'm speaking now of his suicide. I confess that I didn't want to know the details and however it was I came to know of the fact, I didn't read deep into the piece. I don't know how he did it and I would appreciate it if you didn't say anything. But he had been very canny in making of the limitations of his young life—the lack of education, the bullishness of his personality, the few friends—a subject for his writing, and if he had only persevered past the setbacks, discouraging though I'm sure they were, he could've made the limitations of his old age, he could've turned these into the gold of his new books. I have no doubt that he had the skill, the visionary talent. No doubt at all. So he took his life. Which is like a childish tantrum of wanting to show people up. But where does that get you. It doesn't even sound like, from you, that death has given him a very hot spotlight. Warm maybe. Lukewarm, it sounds like. And then it passes. It passes. And you are dead and you have no fight and you're back to the state you lament about. He sighs. I am not a writer so I do not feel as if—nor do I want it—but I certainly do not have the same agency as someone like Laurence. To record his thoughts. To record the wrong that he feels history has done him. I respond. I suggest. Just as intelligently as my writers. That is the way it's always been and I have been happy in this position.

Mr. Levitow, do you mind if I ask you, when you read, besides *The New York Times*, you mentioned names like Roth and Updike, when you read them, is part of you still an editor, marking out sentences or passages for improvement?

Not when I read Roth and Updike, no. These are the masters of the realm. They are the masters our country has yielded. And part of the reason I read them is because I know I will not need to engage that editor's critical mind. I read them for pleasure and for the peace of knowing they cannot be bettered.

Where would you put Laurence in that hierarchy?

I wouldn't, Levitow says.

So you think this biography is not worthwhile? I say, at the same time thinking: Fuck what you think. For the first time all day, I feel the fire of my old self, like hunger, like an ulcer.

No, of course not, Levitow says. Every life is worth documenting. Well, maybe not every life. But Laurence's life certainly is. He does not need to have been a mammoth of American letters to warrant a biography.

So you wouldn't say that Laurence is among the greats of American literature? I ask. Cora Lynn is smiling. If there has been a turn in the conversation, she has missed it entirely. My question comes from the same impulse as aggravating a wound, a childish ploy intending to prolong the pain, the enjoyment of the pain.

No, he most certainly is not. What I will say is that Laurence began very promisingly.

You mean, with your first three books together.

That's right.

But have you read the others he wrote after your relationship ended?

I didn't have any need to. I was no longer his editor.

So how can you say that he didn't make good on what you call his promise.

To be candid, I read an article or two, here and there.

Articles, I say.

And I could tell that his writing hadn't moved much further from when I last encountered it.

Articles, I repeat. But not the books.

Levitow is silent.

On the basis of articles, "here and there," you're prepared to dismiss Laurence?

I don't think I'm dismissing him.

But he is no Roth or Updike or even DeLillo.

Of course not, Levitow says.

Of course not, I say. My tone finally catches Cora Lynn's attention, but other than turning to look at me, she remains noncommittal, still happy to have facilitated this day.

Mr. Levitow may I ask you a question?

He gives a small laugh, as if to say, What have we been doing thus far? Sure, he says.

Do you think Ed Mallory is among the what-you-would-call greats that American literature has produced?

Not Ed, no.

May I ask if you think writing about homosexuality would disqualify you from producing great American literature?

I am not an expert at what you call the genre of gay literature, despite having worked with Laurence on three books. He may be recognized as one of the founders of the genre, but when I was working with him, my concern was to get his voice and his writing to as sharp a place as they could get.

So there are no books written by homosexuals or about homosexuality that you would rank alongside the writers you mentioned?

That's not the way I see the world. I love what I love and I don't have external qualifications for them. Other than excellence and a kind of peace that is induced when you meet excellence.

I think the books Laurence published after he left Norton are greater than those he worked on with you, I say. This is a surprise to me. I hadn't planned on making such a statement. I don't even know if this is what I believe. At least I can be sure of this: those books do not mark a dip in Laurence's writing. Levitow may be right that the first books had a swagger that made you overlook the youthful flaws, the overstatement, the tendency to conflate caricature with characterization. Their autodidact's brio was the making of Laurence. The books that came after, three other novels and a book of essays, were naturally older in spirit, conservative of energy but not politics, with a sourness and cynicism that most readers found off-putting and laid at the feet of his dipping career trajectory but which traits others, myself included, argued had been there all along and had been among his most bracing, welcome writerly qualities, given the times in which they were composed and to which they are addressed. In his books, Laurence spoke like this: *Listen, you motherfuckers … Listen up to my tired, grinding voice, a voice more whine than wine, but that I will turn into my own kind of loner's music, in its odd way not pretty but captivating, and wasted, wasted on all of you undeserving motherfuckers who hear only in the register of cozy life affirmation and banal self-realizations and so on and so forth but I will still speak, I don't know what else to do, and I will still …* and so on and so forth.

I haven't read them, Levitow says.

Yes, that's what you said, I reply. For a moment I had been angry but now I'm just really sad. But look at him, look at Levitow: nearly cross-eyed from the pleasure of sparring. He's alive. Right at this very minute, the most awake he's been in a while, I'd wager. Describing the weather to blind what's-his-name, but otherwise mum, keeping sphinxlike company with one other pensioner in their triumvirate of still-aliveness, observing but not speaking. Saving his talk for the dinner table? He could be the guy who brings everyone up to the twenty-first century. The investment in the computer and in an online *New York Times* subscription pays off center stage during mealtimes: the reciter of the *Times* and the times. Would he spare them the gory parts? How about obituaries? Would they welcome news of their peers' deaths, of death's proximity? He would recite facts, leaving out divisive opinions. Maybe he once provided commentary, before being shouted down: the end of the road, everyone just wants to get along. His eyebrows are aimed at me with fake perturbation but his eyes and some drool at the corner of his mouth are the tells. His mind is so alive. Called to recapitulate his hierarchies, to defend his distinctions, he'd come through, razor-sharp, and I'd been there to see it, so had Cora Lynn. The mind is the first to go? For him it would never be the case. He licks his lips. He wants some more sparring.

So Roth, Updike, Vonnegut, DeLillo. Would you add anyone else to that list?

It wouldn't be much of a list if it got too crowded, Levitow says. Then: Give me names.

Toni Morrison? I say.

No.

No?

I would not put her on that list, Levitow says. She does not belong.

Not even with the Nobel Prize? I say.

If it had been up to me, she would never have gotten it. Undeserving. A sacred cow, Levitow says.

Really? I say, though not a Morrison partisan myself.

Is that the only other name you mean to test me with?

Alice Munro? I ask.

Maybe, Levitow says, and then changes his mind. No. I don't know enough of her work to be able to judge.

But not Laurence, I repeat.

Laurence Warshow is not on that list, young man.

Despite the fact that you called him visionary. A visionary talent.

He is not on that list, Levitow says again.

David Foster Wallace?

I don't know his work.

Jonathan Franzen?

I've only read one book. I liked it. But I'm not prepared to call him one of the greats based on one work alone.

Cora Lynn had been turning her head from one face to another during this litany, as if she was at a tennis match. The smile has not once left her face. What is this game anyway? The Oracle at Queen of Angels?

Sitting here, I realize: I won't keep my promise. I will not mail Laurence's books to Levitow. There is no reason for coming back. He is a man of his time, happy in his deathless ideas. He will wait for my call or for Cora Lynn's. In a week, in two, not hearing from me through Cora Lynn, he will have softened his certainties. He'll be prepared to maybe, just *maybe*, induct Laurence into his club of eternals, but situating Laurence in an antechamber, not yet fit to enter, but at least within begging distance. He'll say anything I want to hear just so I will return and again give him this rare time. Refuting feckless multiculturalism with ideas of which he is neither progenitor nor, with his aged body, perpetuator. But being deathless, these ideas will outlive him. *That is what this young man does not understand.* These are ideas being held not just by him—he is merely one of the flame-bearers. In front and next to him, so many more: plus one and one and yet another … With me, today, he gets the chance to be deathless.

About the Author

Han Ong is the author of the novels *Fixer Chao* and *The Disinherited*. A MacArthur Fellow, he was most recently awarded the Berlin Prize from the American Academy in Berlin. His new play *Grandeur* will have its world premiere at San Francisco's Magic Theatre in the Spring of 2017.

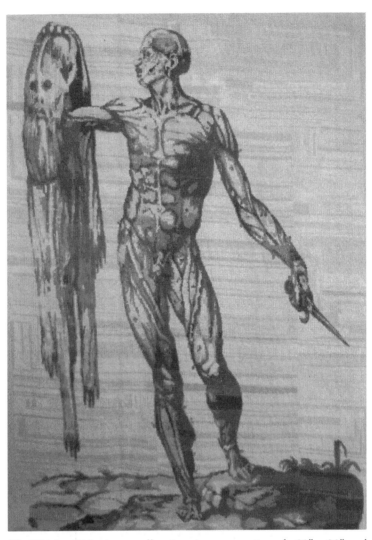

The Weight of Man is a needlepoint piece, approximately 29" x 22" and composed entirely of linen canvas and cotton thread.

About the Artist: Holly Day has taught writing classes at the Loft Literary Center in Minnesota since 2000. Her published books include *Music Theory for Dummies*, *Music Composition for Dummies*, *Guitar All-in-One for Dummies*, *Piano All-in-One for Dummies*, *Walking Twin*

Cities, *Insider's Guide to the Twin Cities*, *Nordeast Minneapolis: A History*, and *The Book Of*, while her poetry has recently appeared in *New Ohio Review*, *SLAB*, and *Gargoyle*. Her newest poetry book, *Ugly Girl*, just came out from Shoe Music Press.

Visit www.yourimpossiblevoice.com for information on our next issue, submission guidelines, and recordings of our authors reading their work.

45927221R00080

Made in the USA
Middletown, DE
17 July 2017